"Yes, Mr. Darcy"

A Pride & Prejudice Variation

J. DAWN KING

Yes, Mr. Darcy

This is a work of fiction. The characters, locations, and
events portrayed in this book are fictitious or are used
fictitiously. Any similarity to real persons, living or dead is
purely coincidental and not intended by the author.

Cover: JD Smith – Design
Cover photography © Richard Jenkins 2016
Interior Formatting: Anibal Renán Ramirez

Published by Joy D. King

Print ISBN-13: 978-0-9975376-1-1
Print ISBN-10: 0-9975376-1-2

Library of Congress Control Number - 2016906671

ACKNOWLEDGEMENTS

My sincerest thanks goes to the editing team of Debbie Fortin and Anji Dale. Do you realize you are the most patient individuals on the planet? You are.

This project is my first novella length story. I found out during the process of developing this tale that I am, as my husband and mother have accused me of on more than one occasion, wordy. Who knew? Well, my husband and mom did, of course.

Richard Jenkins, you proved to be a miracle worker. After weeks of searching online for an appropriate cover image, I found your site and almost swooned with the quality and variety of your work. You, too, proved to be patient as together we chose the best Lizzy Bennet. Isn't she lovely? Sigh!

Finally, to the many readers who left hundreds of comments and reviews on fanfiction.net. You rock!!!

Yes, Mr. Darcy

To my Mom—with affection and love. I'm proud to be
your daughter.

TABLE OF CONTENTS

CHAPTER ONE

Elizabeth Bennet knew heartbreak when she heard it. She had listened to its mournful wails from her mother each time a birth resulted in a daughter rather than the needed son. The expected joy turning to hopelessness when the midwife announced the sex. Years after the last child was born, Elizabeth had sobbed when her father finally explained to his favorite daughter the circumstances of the entail on their home, which they would lose to a relative stranger if a son was not to be had. It was the first of many small cracks in Elizabeth's heart.

She had witnessed the depths of despair when her eldest sister shed salty tears as another year passed and no suitor came to Longbourn asking for her hand. The sweetest sister in the world with no hope caused the cracks to splinter, like a pane of glass that did not shatter on impact—where the fracture spread out like a bolt of lightning across a cloud-covered sky.

Her own dear father's demand that Elizabeth marry Longbourn's heir to protect her mother and sisters was an arrow that pierced the remains of her distressed organ. She was crushed. The visit to Derbyshire with her beloved aunt and uncle was to be her last opportunity for freedom before the marriage was arranged. Until this point in their travels, Elizabeth had been able to force the future from her thinking. Hearing the woman cry brought it all back. Yes, Elizabeth Bennet knew heartbreak.

The lady standing in the churchyard was younger than Elizabeth had assumed. She was dressed finely in pastel colors. Elizabeth was surprised to find there was no black; the grief seemed fresh. Yet the headstone was weathered and elegantly carved, attesting to the passage of time since the loved one died. *Was it a parent? A brother or sister? A mate?*

The Gardiners, accompanied by their niece, had arrived in Lambton the day prior. Madeline Gardiner had grown up in the small market town and had been pleased when her husband offered her the opportunity to visit old friends. Days of travel had left Elizabeth feeling restless, something she would mend with a walk through the village into the countryside. This was already the third trip from one end of the town to the other. Touring the small town took very little time.

The cemetery was beside an old stone church which looked to have been in place for centuries. It was solid, with climbing ivy surrounding each window opening as if trying to spy on those who attended services—and account for those who did not. Black wrought-iron gates, standing open, invited the curious and those suffering a loss. The young girl appeared to be the latter.

Elizabeth was more than curious. She felt the young miss's pain in her own heart. The girl appeared to be the same age as her youngest sister, Lydia. *How could she not offer assistance?* She approached quietly, stopping only to gather some wildflowers growing by the gate.

When she reached the girl's side, she extended the hand clasping the blossoms. It caught the attention of the mourner. Embarrassed at being found in tears, the young lady put her finely embroidered handkerchief to use. Then she reached for the posy.

With not a word spoken, she knelt to place the flowers on the grave. Elizabeth looked to the carving. One year to the day.

"Mrs. Mildred Northam"
Born 2 May 1734
Died 30 July 1810
"Beloved Nurse and Companion"

"Would you mind telling me about Mrs. Northam? Was she a kindly woman? Did she enjoy children?" Elizabeth whispered her questions. She was pleased when the girl turned her eyes towards her. They were brilliant blue. Kind, troubled eyes.

"She was the wisest woman I have ever known. When my mother passed at my birth, Mrs. Northam cared for me as if I was her own. Though elderly, she was spry and inventive and imaginative—everything a little girl could possibly want in a friend. She had tended my brother before me and my father as well so Norty was family." The young girl sighed. "My brother wanted to place her alongside our parents in the family crypt. However, before she died she insisted on being outside in the sunshine. Nature was her greatest pleasure." The girl's chest heaved, the sigh more audible than the sobs had been. "I have missed her presence many times over the last year, but never more so than now."

"May I offer my sympathies to you?" Elizabeth was sincere. She could see by the girl's countenance that she was a gentle soul. With the loss of her parents and the mention of only one brother, who may not have been much older, this sad young lady was alone. Elizabeth sought to share her pain, a way to emotionally meet on common ground. "All of my grandparents are gone. It has been many years, but I miss them still." She moved a bit closer, within arms distance. "My aunt, uncle, and I are merely passing through these parts, so you may speak to me with impunity should you like. I have four sisters and no brother at home. I know how much it helps to speak of grief." Elizabeth took another small step towards her. "Might I share your burden?"

It was boldly done. However, the facts could not be denied. Elizabeth would remain in Lambton for no more than three days before pressing home to Hertfordshire and the misery which awaited her. For some reason, hearing someone else's sorrow eased her own.

"You would do this for a stranger?" The girl was bewildered.

Elizabeth smiled at her and asked, "Would you not do it for me?"

The girl paused for only a moment before directing Elizabeth to a bench placed at the edge of the cemetery.

"I grew up but a few miles from here. My brother is much older than me and has been more like a father for the past five years since the death of Papa. His friend and companion while he was growing up showed me special attention while I was at the seaside this summer." The tears again started falling. "I acted as a foolish child." Her breath shuddered in and out. "I convinced myself that he loved me. However, it was my dowry which caught and held his attention. Nothing else."

Elizabeth reached over and placed her hand on the young girl's. "I am deeply sorry. You must have been devastated when you realized his treachery."

The girl bowed her head, her chin almost touching her chest. "I was." She sniffed inelegantly. Elizabeth smiled, touched that the young lady was so comfortable in her presence. "A million times I have wished Norty was here."

"What do you believe she would do if she was?"

"She would hold me and scold me and remind me how young I am. Then she would call me a silly girl and tell me to wipe my tears and then have me walk with her in the gardens on the south lawn with the tall oak trees so I would realize how small my problems are in comparison to the world around me."

Elizabeth softly chuckled at the haste with which the girl spoke. "Ah, she sounds a wise woman."

"Oh, she was exceedingly wise. It was as if she knew what I was thinking before I thought it." The girl chuckled as well. "One time, when I was but ten years of age, I had been spending much time in the gallery in our home, studying the portrait of my mother. My brother is dark-haired like Papa and I have my mother's straw-colored hair. My father used to call me a miniature of her. However, it was not their faces that interested me. My mother's clothing and hair intrigued me. Before I could mention my interest, Norty had brought down one of my mother's ball gowns and dressed me up to be a small replica, tall powdered hair and all."

The girl laughed. "I looked atrocious. There were not enough pins at Pemberley to make the dress do anything other than hang on me and the powder kept getting into my nose and making me sneeze each time I moved my head. When I asked to have it removed, Norty told me I had to wear it downstairs to dinner, just as my mother had done. Unfortunately, my brother was home from university and was witness to my foolishness." She sighed with the memory. "He did not laugh like I thought he would. Instead, he offered me his arm, as if I was a grown up lady, and escorted me to the dining room." She giggled.

Elizabeth smiled along with her, grateful the girl was

sharing a treasured event from her youth.

"It was my first time eating out of the nursery. However, each time I moved my head to take a bite of soup, white debris would drop into the bowl. Fitzwilliam and I both received a stern look from Papa at the laughter neither of us could contain and I was asked to return upstairs and dress appropriately. My brother helped me from my seat as the dress was a challenge to walk in, bowed to me, and then escorted me upstairs. He called me, 'my lady'. A tray was brought up and he ate with me, his big form bent double trying to fit on one of the small chairs. Norty laughed at us both. She never minded a bit of mischief from either of us and she always understood why we wanted what we did."

"I comprehend your love of such an incredible woman." Elizabeth smiled at her.

"She was special in every way." The girl's eyes looked to the skyline beyond the cemetery, lost to years past.

"Then might I ask again: What instruction do you believe she would give you now?"

"I do not know." The answer came fast.

Elizabeth waited.

"Oh, I do know." For the first time the girl looked directly at Elizabeth. "She would remind me that I am not yet sixteen and have two years before I am ready to be out in society. Norty would reason with me until I figured out whatever lessons I had learned from my decisions. She would then inquire, bluntly, I might add, when I would get around to learning them."

It had been the same with Elizabeth's father. He appreciated curiosity, but he thrived on improving Elizabeth's understanding of what made the world go around, what her place was on the earth, and how she could benefit herself and others by living there.

"So I will ask you, since your dear Norty is not here, what lesson did you learn?"

The girl pondered and Elizabeth could see she was giving the matter her full attention.

"Before this summer, I did not fully appreciate my own value, my heritage. Our family is gentry and I am the granddaughter of an earl. Had my brother not rescued me before it was too late and had my actions become known, I would have been solely responsible for damaging my family name. Norty taught me how to behave properly. I know the rules of society. Nevertheless, I allowed myself to believe that love justified breaking the rules. I was wrong."

"Solely responsible? What about the young man?"

"Yes, he was wrong in approaching me, trying to take advantage of my ignorance and innocence. Nonetheless, because of his position in society, the repercussion would have come back on me, not him."

"I am sure you are correct." Elizabeth again reached over and patted the back of her hand. "Since I am assuming it has not become known, what will you do the next time a young man professes his love? How will you act?"

"I will not put my trust in my own emotions as I know my heart is treacherous." She stiffened her spine and lifted her chin. "My brother and my cousin, who both serve as my guardians, are intelligent men. I will trust their judgement from now on."

"Then, Norty is here, miss." Elizabeth glanced back to the grave. "The principles she instilled and the closeness you felt is still within you. It will never leave you as long as you remember her voice." Elizabeth asked, "Has your brother said as much to you?"

"I cannot bear to look at him to see his disappointment." She whispered as her chin dropped again. "He inherited the weight of responsibly managing our estate and the care of me. I have caused him no end of pain because of what I have done." Tears dripped on the front of her dress.

A deep voice spoke from behind them. "Never, dearest."

Both Elizabeth and the young lady turned. Before them was a handsome man dressed in fine clothing. His chiseled face was without expression, though his eyes were filled with sorrow.

"Fitzwilliam!" The girl stood and ran to his opened arms. "However did you find me?"

He hugged her to him, whispering soft words of reassurance, and rested his cheek on the top of her bonnet. "Where else would you be, Georgie?"

Elizabeth could not take her eyes away from them. So much pain for two people so alone. Remembering her own troubles, she was surprised at her longing to climb inside those strong arms and hear his promises of comfort.

The young girl needed her no longer. Standing, she quietly left the graveyard, knowing she would never see them again.

CHAPTER TWO

Fitzwilliam Darcy was perplexed. Where could she have gone?

He had diligently searched Lambton for the woman who had provided solace and imparted such keen insight to Georgiana, to no avail. She seemed to have vanished into the air. For months, each time he had ridden through the small hamlet, his eyes examined the footpaths and the shops. Yet he did not find her.

When he had taken Georgiana to London to resume her studies with the masters, he looked there as well. Many times over the past months he regretted not speaking up, not seeking an introduction. But it was not the time nor the place to have done so. The words the young woman uttered to his sister had started the process of healing so that Georgiana was restored to him. Her confidence in her ability to make decisions and to be independent had blossomed. Darcy owed the woman his undying gratitude.

Everywhere he went, he searched. Eventually, he hoped in his heart that if he looked long enough and hard enough, he would find her.

Finally, he did.

The autumn assembly in the market town of Meryton was held in a crowded room attached to the inn. Darcy's party was late arriving. The music was almost ready to start.

She stood before him, her face as beautiful as he remembered. But her eyes...gone was the kind intelligence and the flash of life he had observed when she had comforted his sister. In their place he saw misery of the acutest kind. He recognized her mask, the impenetrable shield worn in public so observers could not see the pain and agony of heart that threatened to overwhelm her. He wondered at the cause.

Elizabeth Bennet. A regal name for a queenly countenance.

He bowed. Before he did, he spied the flicker of recognition.

"Mr. Darcy," the screech of the woman's mother, heard above the musicians tuning their instruments before beginning the dance, drew his eyes back from where they longed to remain. "You have yet to meet my husband's cousin, Mr. William Collins, rector of Hunsford, who serves under the patronage of Lady Catherine de Bourgh, a grand woman of substantial means. Mr. Bennet and I hope that soon we will have a much closer familial relationship, with both the Lady and our cousin—when a particular blessed event takes place."

Darcy was horrified to see Mrs. Bennet look towards Elizabeth as the means of establishing that closer relationship. *She was taken?*

Darcy's eyes shot to the man standing far too close to the young woman. He knew him. In the spring when he had visited his aunt's home, Rosings Park in Kent, the rector had been newly installed in the living his aunt held. It had taken only a few minutes to know the man as a groveling sycophant who sought to please his patroness, rather than the God he had sworn to serve.

The first words from the rector's mouth failed to change Darcy's opinion.

"Mr. Darcy, I am astonished you are in Hertfordshire!" Mr. Collins bowed and spoke at the same time. "As a near relation to my patroness, it is my pleasure to inform you that both your aunt, Lady Catherine de Bourgh, and your cousin, Miss Anne de Bourgh, were in good health when I left Kent. They often condescend to..."

As the clergyman started to ramble on in the manner he had done when he was last in his company, Darcy, again, caught the eye of the young woman. *Mr. Collins was her pain. Were they engaged to marry? Was that the happy event her mother referred to?* A sick feeling crept into his stomach at the thought. He did the only thing he could think of at the time.

"Miss Elizabeth, if you are available, might I request the honor of the first set?"

He saw it. Relief flashed across her face before she was able to pull it back to the stoic calm she had offered the room before. It was enough.

"Yes, Mr. Darcy." She curtseyed and accepted his arm as the musicians were preparing to start the next song. They walked to the front of the line.

He heard the squawks of Caroline Bingley and Louisa Hurst, his host's sisters, as they noticed his position on the floor. From experience, Darcy knew they were aware he rarely danced with someone outside of those in his party and he never danced the first set. He looked down the line and caught his friend Charles Bingley's notice. Bingley danced with Elizabeth's older sister. Darcy was surprised the man was able to look away from the lovely woman across from him. He read the signs — Bingley was in love, again.

Darcy watched Bingley's response at seeing him so engaged. The younger man turned his attention from Miss Bennet and broke out into a smile — a normal posture for Charles.

It had not been Darcy's desire to attend the assembly at Meryton. He had arrived from London a few hours before the party needed to leave and barely had time to bathe and change before they departed from Bingley's leased estate, Netherfield Park. Being in attendance while only knowing those in his party was a challenge to a man who did not fare well in social settings. However, as he had for the past few months, he sought opportunity to locate the missing maiden. He had gone to balls, soirees, card parties, performances—all in hopes of spotting the one woman he longed to meet. Darcy smiled to himself at finally achieving success.

***

Elizabeth Bennet had never felt such gratitude. Mr. Collins had failed to request the first set, possibly assuming he would be gifted such a privilege without having to ask. He was a large, clumsy man who all the Bennet sisters, including kind, sweet Jane, hoped they would not be partnered with for even one dance. Both Mr. and Mrs. Bennet had taken Elizabeth aside before the carriage had arrived to transport them to the ball, and reminded her of her duty to the family.

The frustration that had budded when they had first demanded of her that she marry a stranger, had blossomed into anger at her father for not caring for the futures of his five daughters. Instead he had crawled into his bookroom and stayed there. He provided no instruction to his offspring, no restraint over the financial demands of his wife, and no alternative to the eventual loss of their home. The injustice of sacrificing her hopes and dreams to benefit a mother who cared for her own future at the expense of her second, least favorite daughter, chafed at her.

From the minute the express had been delivered to her at Lambton, demanding her immediate return to Longbourn for the purpose of meeting the heir, she had been distraught. Yes, during those months, she had thought often of the young girl and her brother, wishing again for those strong arms that had so carefully held his sister to give her comfort from her present dilemma. Now that he stood across from her, she knew it was too late. Just prior to leaving her home for the assembly, Mr. Collins had requested to speak with her privately after they broke their fast the next morning. He would propose marriage and her fate would be sealed. She exhaled a breath she had not realized she had been holding.

"Miss Elizabeth, have you known Mr. Collins long?" It was a bold question from a new acquaintance.

"Sir, I was called away early from Lambton to meet my father's heir."

"His heir?"

"Our estate, Longbourn, is entailed and Mr. Collins will be the beneficiary upon my father's eventual death." She spoke quickly before the dance pattern parted them.

As soon as Darcy approached her again, he asked. "How well known is he to you?"

"You likely have more knowledge of the man than I, Mr. Darcy." Elizabeth debated with herself before providing additional information. Sharing personal details with someone of recent introduction broke a fundamental rule of propriety. Nevertheless, Darcy had witnessed his sister exposing sensitive events in her life to Elizabeth so she felt comfortable doing the same with him.

"He had written in the spring to request the hand of one of the five daughters of the Bennet household and my parents, while I was traveling, chose me." She did not mean to gulp in a breath, though her words were rushed and her breathing shallow. "He arrived in Hertfordshire shortly after my departure for Derbyshire and stayed for a se'nnight. When I returned to Longbourn, there was only one day remaining of his stay. Apparently it was enough time for him to determine his future—and mine."

"Is not Miss Bennet the eldest?" The expression on his face was puzzled.

"My mother has long intended for my eldest sister, Jane, to marry a gentleman of substance, quite like you, sir. My younger sisters are not yet ready to run a home. Therefore, my journey with my aunt and uncle to the north was to allow me the opportunity to come to terms with my prospects."

"And have you done so?"

She looked into his eyes, surprised at the seriousness she found there. He was not taking this conversation lightly. Elizabeth closed her eyes for a brief moment. Decorum demanded they speak of the weather or the roads. However, she could not begin to broach such mundane subjects with this man.

"I have not."

***

Darcy pondered her answer. She could not be a mercenary woman or she would have welcomed an arranged marriage of convenience. This certainly set her out as outstandingly different from the women of his acquaintance.

He did not fool himself into believing the women of the ton and beyond had sought him for anything other than his wealth and respected name. None of them knew the man, only the money. In the eight years he had been on the marriage market, he had been proposed to, propositioned, and coerced by mothers, fathers, uncles, and grandparents alike to increase their fortunes and influence by attaching their female relatives to him. He was bone-weary of their efforts.

The music continued as they moved in time with the other dancers. For a length of time the pattern kept them close.

"How is your sister, sir? Is she recovered much?"

Again, Darcy offered a small smile. That Elizabeth could think of someone else at this time spoke much about her character. It was as he expected — she understood the turmoil in his sister's heart.

"I am pleased to tell you that she is on the way to being much as she was before you met." He saw her relief. "No, I misspoke. She is much improved and has determined to become a young lady of character and discernment. I believe the both of us have you to thank for this awareness, Miss Elizabeth."

She blushed at his words.

"While I appreciate your kindness in saying so, I believe the influence of her governess guaranteed she would, in time, rise above the circumstances which confronted her this summer." Her smile was genuine. "I was merely a listening ear."

"Not so, Miss Elizabeth." Darcy's voice was soft, but firm. "She repeated almost verbatim your conversation. I found your expressions to be wise." A phrase from a poem he had recently read came to mind.

'That best portion of a good man's life, his little, nameless, unremembered, acts of kindness and of love.'

He had no idea he had whispered the words aloud until Elizabeth responded, "Lyrical Ballads."

"You are a reader of Wordsworth then?" Darcy was surprised at a female's familiarity with the poem.

"Your condescension is showing, Mr. Darcy." Her soft laugh was far superior to his ear than the stringed instruments playing to the crowded assembly.

It was his turn to blush. "Just so, madam."

"In repayment of the gift you bestowed upon my family, Miss Elizabeth, I offer all the resources in my possession to help you out of your current situation. You need only ask."

Elizabeth sucked in a breath. She knew from the cut of their clothes and the manner in which they comported themselves, that the Darcys were wealthy. When she had asked her aunt Gardiner if she was familiar with the family, she had been told they held one of the largest estates in England. What he proposed was exceedingly magnanimous. It was beyond her to accept.

"Upon my word, Mr. Darcy, what a generous offer to be made to a stranger, though I cannot imagine what you might be able to do." The sparkle in her eyes and the smile on her face belied her words. She would not take advantage. The sigh almost shook her slight frame. "My kindness was not done for repayment, sir."

"Of that fact I am aware." Yes, this woman was unlike any he had ever met. He thought of how Miss Caroline Bingley would have responded to his offer. Charles' unmarried sister had pursued him with ferocity in an effort to become the next mistress of his home, Pemberley. He continued to stare at Elizabeth as they moved slowly through the dance. She was not Caroline Bingley and he was grateful.

"Will you accept him then?" Darcy almost could not breathe, his trepidation threatened to overwhelm him.

"I know what is expected of me, sir." Her look was fierce, though it rapidly changed to sadness. "I have not yet reached my majority so have little opportunity of going against the wishes of my parents. The portion which will be left to me and my sisters is small. We have only our charms to recommend us. Until Mr. Collins, even that has not been enough to induce an offer which would have been... more palatable."

Darcy deeply appreciated her frankness. He would return the favor.

"Do you walk out in the mornings, Miss Elizabeth?" He hoped her stroll at Lambton was not an anomaly.

"Yes, Mr. Darcy." Thinking quickly, she made a decision. "There is a stile halfway between Longbourn and Netherfield Park. I shall proceed in its direction at first light."

The set had ended. He took her hand and bowed over it, whispering so only she could hear, "I will be there."

CHAPTER THREE

The morning sun was a hazy outline on the horizon when Darcy arrived at the stile. He easily spotted her approach.

"Miss Elizabeth." Her cheeks were red from the early morning chill, a direct contrast with the dull colors of her dress and pelisse. Darcy felt a rush of pleasure as he realized she had not sought to please him by dressing up in her finest. It could not have been her goal to impress him, though she did just the same.

"Mr. Darcy."

They both smiled at the ridiculousness of being polite under the circumstances. If they were caught together, the consequences could be dire for both of them. Darcy realized a compromise might be an answer to her prayers., though the idea of her being married to a man she knew little about had to be unappealing — though not as unappealing as being wed to Mr. Collins.

"You requested this meeting, sir. I cannot help but wonder if you have a plan?"

Darcy suspected that Elizabeth Bennet had a quick mind and strong opinions. He wondered if she had an independent spirit and realized he would be the recipient of that information as soon as he shared his purpose in meeting her.

"Miss Elizabeth, I not only have a plan that I believe will temporarily allow you to think of and pursue other avenues, I have taken it upon myself to already set events in motion."

"How can that be, sir?" He could see she was astounded and upset. Darcy realized he was not known to her, nor was he in possession of any authority over her. It had to rankle that she had not been consulted. He would not have been at all surprised had Elizabeth stomped her foot at him. He would have done so and so would have Georgiana.

It was as he expected. Fiercely independent. No wonder she balked so at being tied to a toad.

Darcy raised his palms in peace. "It needed to be so, Miss Elizabeth, to avoid having you placed in a position where you would have to respond to an offer from your father's cousin."

***

He was dressed entirely in black — a somber color which reflected, Elizabeth assumed, his normal countenance in company. Though she had witnessed small moments of amusement the night before, she inherently knew they were rare. He seemed an intelligent man and she hoped his superior knowledge of the ways of the world outside Hertfordshire might provide her relief.

Elizabeth turned from him and walked rapidly in a small circle, chewing on her thumbnail as she went. *Was he planning to kidnap Mr. Collins and have him transported to Australia? Was he going to kidnap her so she could not return to Longbourn and face the rector? Was he proposing to run off with her to Gretna Green?* She shook her head at her far-fetched ideas. Mr. Darcy may *think* he was in her debt, but, in fact, he was not.

Inhaling deeply, she stopped her furious movement and stood directly in front of him. Exhaling, she finally replied, "Mr. Darcy, I am ready to hear your plan."

***

"First, you must know that my aunt, Lady Catherine de Bourgh, has long held that I have had a 'peculiar' engagement with her daughter, Anne." He held his hand up when Elizabeth started to speak. "I do not, Miss Elizabeth. It is a fabrication of her vivid imagination which she stubbornly clings to. I will not marry my cousin, nor does she have any desire to marry me."

Now, it was his turn to move restlessly about the paddock.

"When this idea was first presented to me by Lady Catherine after the loss of my father, I refused to acquiesce — quite firmly." He breathed in and out quickly in his frustration, removing his hat and twisting the brim in his large hands. "To no avail. In the years since my father's death, Lady Catherine has chosen to repeat her desires to the extent that she now fully believes them to be, not only her will, but that of my deceased mother as well."

Finally, he stopped back in front of Elizabeth.

"My point of telling you this, Miss Elizabeth, is that in my frustration at her continually bringing the matter to my attention, I refused to answer her for the past three years." Darcy started tapping his hat against his thigh. "When she spoke of it or demanded that I take the action of making an offer to Anne, I pretended to ignore her." He scoffed at himself. "Oh, I know how mature that makes me sound, however, it was my way of retaining control of my temper. She is my aunt after all."

"I do comprehend the difficulties of family members who put their own concerns ahead of yours, sir."

"Lady Catherine relishes power and control. Her desire to have me for a son-in-law is for the sole purpose of combining her estate with mine, therefore becoming the largest private landowner in England. It is for that purpose only that she seeks to marry her daughter to me." Darcy huffed out a breath, the vapor projecting into the air and disappearing into the mist. "Her love for control is not solely for this issue. She demands and receives absolute obedience from her rector. She expects him to serve her and be available at her whim. With that in mind, I wrote a letter to Lady Catherine last night when I returned to Netherfield Park and had it sent by express already this morning saying I would not be marrying Anne and that I have found a young woman of interest. It will be in her hands by this evening."

Elizabeth put her hand to her chest. "A young woman of interest?"

"Yes, Miss Elizabeth." Darcy looked directly into her eyes.

"Oh, Mr. Darcy. From what you have told me and what I have gleaned from Mr. Collins, Lady Catherine will be livid."

"That she will, Miss Elizabeth." Darcy shuddered at the thought. He did not fear his aunt, but he knew firsthand how the woman's anger had far-reaching effects, like an ocean wave pounding against a rocky shore, dislodging heavy boulders until it changed a distant coastline.

He continued. "This morning, I will not return to Netherfield Park, but will present myself to Mr. Collins at your home. Once I explain what I have done, I will beg for his immediate return to Kent to be of comfort to my aunt. I cannot see how the man would allow any other concern to take precedence over his need to attend Lady Catherine." Darcy looked into her lovely eyes and saw hope. "Thus, if you time your return until after I have spent a few moments with Mr. Collins, I do believe you will be free of his attentions until we can come up with an alternative plan."

"But what of your aunt, sir? If she thinks you have an interest in a young woman not her daughter, will she not attempt to find her for the purpose of causing dissension?" He heard her concern.

"Yes, it is exactly how I expect events to take place, but do not be anxious." Darcy tried to reassure her. "I am my own master."

"Sir, she will come to Hertfordshire, will she not?"

"I imagine so."

"And she will find you have formed no attachment to a lady." As soon as she said it, she put her hand to her mouth. "Sir, I offer my apologies. In my concern for my own problems, I wrongly assumed you were speaking of me. I failed to give credence to the possibility of you courting Miss Bingley. If Miss Bingley becomes aware of our meeting this morning or the extent you are going to provide assistance to me, it could cause difficulty. I am truly sorry."

He was shocked. *She thought he was courting Caroline Bingley?* He shuddered again, shaking his head as he did so. *Never!*

"No, Miss Elizabeth, I am *not* attached to Miss Bingley." He was quick to reassure her and realized it reassured himself as well. *Never!* He exhaled quickly getting back on point. "It is my opinion that Lady Catherine will direct Mr. Collins to focus his attentions elsewhere rather than on the

Bennet family if she sees that I am taken with you."

"But you are not 'taken' with me, sir." Elizabeth's breathing quickened and a blush appeared on her cheeks.

"Am I not?" He could not keep from smiling.

***

Elizabeth's heart thundered at the thought that he might actually be attracted to her. He was all that a young man should be. His kindness drew her to him and gave her hope of future felicity. He was compassionate towards his sister and honorable towards her. The last thought gave her pause. Yes, he was chivalrous enough to seek her best interest ahead of his own. Never had she met a man like him.

But, why? Why would he rouse the expectations of both his relatives and hers? She carefully pondered his motives. Suddenly it dawned on her.

She took a small step closer. "Oh, you!" She could see what he was up to. "You are a calculating man, Mr. Darcy. For if Lady Catherine, with Mr. Collins in tow, comes to Longbourn, she will take her anger out on me as well as you. However, if we stand together as one, she will be forced to accept your point, that you will not marry her daughter. I will be without an offer of marriage by Mr. Collins as he would not go against his patroness. Thus, we will both, after the initial confrontation with your aunt, be free of unwanted entanglements."

It was a good plan. It bothered her not that she would face the ire of such a great lady. She would do anything to not have to marry Mr. Collins.

"As well, since this was of your doing, my father and mother will be disappointed at the loss of such a prospect, but their anger will not be directed towards me. My mother, in particular, would never expect a man of your stature to show any interest to any daughter other than Jane so there would be no fear of her trying attach my name to yours." Elizabeth paused as she considered the consequences of such a course. "Once this is done, you can depart from Hertfordshire as a free man, sir. You will have performed a service to me, which you feel you owe due to my kindness to Miss Darcy. We will be even. Justice will have been served." She clasped her hands together and a smile lit her face. "What a master plan you have thought of, Mr. Darcy. Superior!"

Her mask settled firmly into place.

Elizabeth's heart ached. Having him leave without any hope of seeing him again was suddenly excruciating. Unexpectedly, she wanted to cry rather than smile. In truth, she yearned for her name to be connected to his. Elizabeth remembered how he had held his sister at the churchyard. He had personal qualities that appealed to her as no other had. She longed to sigh, to clasp her arms over her chest to ward off the pain. She did not. Elizabeth had to accept that her future was even more uncertain than before.

***

He appreciated her quick mind. She had worked out the finer details and calculated the expected results of putting this into action.

"We can, then, let our families know there will be no courtship between us." Elizabeth spoke, her voice sounding flat to his ears.

"There will not?" He was surprised at the emotions surging through his chest at the thought. *Where had that come from?*

Her head tilted to the side, a look of confusion on her face. Then she laughed. "You are teasing me, sir. You are a great man of elevated rank and I am merely a country gentleman's daughter. For a certainty there would be no courtship."

Elizabeth's laughter stilled when she noted he had not joined in her merriment. She shook her head and her voice became quieter as she spoke, her face looking at the ground. "I misspoke, did I not?" She looked directly at him. "I do not understand."

***

She was a young woman of courage and valor. In Derbyshire and both times in Hertfordshire when Darcy had occasion to be with her he learned qualities and characteristics that appealed to him. She had integrity, something he had been taught by his father to cherish in another man. He never thought to find it in a woman.

"Miss Elizabeth, it is my turn to offer my apologies." He reached over and touched her arm, surprising even him. He had never touched a woman unrelated to him in such a way. "You were quite correct in your assumption of how I expect matters to take place. That you have been made to feel unworthy, in any way, was not my intention." Darcy wondered at how to express the thought that was streaming through his brain and wished for Bingley's easy ability with words. "I am a gentleman and you are a gentleman's daughter. Thus, we are equal. I would be delighted, and so would my sister, if we could count you as a friend."

He wondered how she would respond.

"A friend." She whispered.

Darcy waited.

Elizabeth's chin lifted and resolution shot from her eyes. She smiled up at him. "Then, Mr. Darcy, I shall deliberately slow my walk this morning so I return to Longbourn after you have had opportunity to speak with my father's cousin." She stepped towards him and curtseyed. "Safe travels, Mr. Darcy. I shall see you at my home."

He took her hand and bowed over it, wondering if she felt the sparks that flew between them as soon as his gloved hand touched hers. *What had happened here?*

CHAPTER FOUR

"Mr. Darcy to see you, sir."

William Collins had taken a large portion of the sliced ham and shoved it in his mouth immediately prior to Darcy being announced. The presence of the wad of food caused him such incertitude that, in the end, he did nothing. He did not chew, nor did he swallow. The rector sat with his mouth open. To an onlooker, it was an unpleasant sight.

Mr. Hill rolled his eyes and grabbed a chamber pot from the cupboard kept in the dining room for the men to use when the ladies were dismissed after a meal. The servant wiped the dust from the rim and presented it to the clergyman.

"Stand away!" Once he had been relieved of the mass of meat, Mr. Collins yelled his command at the man who had come to his aid. "What are you about? Do you not know that the nephew of my patroness is awaiting me?" He stood so rapidly the chair threatened to tip backwards, but was saved by the steady hands of the butler. "Do you not understand, man? For such a great man to seek me out so early in the day, there must be a matter of some urgency that begs for my humble expertise." Mr. Collins smacked his lips together and stood taller at the thought of Mr. Darcy being reliant on his good counsel.

Mr. Hill did indeed step aside and watched the rector march purposefully into the drawing room. He shook his head and went about his duties.

***

"Mr. Darcy, you have come seeking advice? Spiritual wisdom?" Mr. Collins started bowing to the taller man as soon as he entered the room. It was an odd sort of movement, this stepping forward and bending at the waist, reminiscent of a hen bobbing its head up and down as it scratched and pecked at the ground for food.

Darcy waited until Mr. Collins stood in front of him. *The nerve of the man! Seeking advice or counsel from a fool? Never!* "Be seated, Mr. Collins. I have a matter concerning my aunt which, I believe, requires your immediate attention."

He sat.

"Mr. Darcy, you should know I would do anything within my power to aid my patroness. I feel the pain of my neglect of being in her presence most acutely. Anything you say is my first priority." Mr. Collins attempted to bow again, his movements ungainly in his seated position.

"By this evening, Lady Catherine will receive a letter by express stating my intention to pursue a courtship with a lady other than my cousin, Anne de Bourgh."

"But, sir!"

"It has solely been Lady Catherine who planned a marriage between Anne and myself. I am my own master and Anne has never wanted to remove herself from Rosings to my home in Derbyshire."

"But, sir!" He raised his right hand and sat forward on the chair.

"Though I understand you are in Hertfordshire to pursue your own happiness by establishing an engagement with one of your cousin's daughters, I am convinced that, under these circumstances, Lady Catherine would not condone you putting your own desires ahead of her needs, do you not agree?"

"Certainly, sir. But..." Mr. Collins put both hands on the arms of his chair as if to launch himself from it at the first opportunity.

"Furthermore, since you are the person who would be last in my company, I feel my aunt will interrogate you for details of my decision, thus I ask that you pay particular attention as I do not want to repeat myself."

Darcy continued with the information he had prepared on the short ride after seeing Elizabeth. It had been his intention to convince Mr. Collins that Elizabeth would not be a good wife for a minister who was under the thumb of his aunt, thus motivating him to refuse to offer for her. However, he could not speak of her in such a way.

"Both my sister and I have been acquainted with the young woman for several months. We met in Derbyshire. She is my equal." He paused thinking of the qualities he admired in Elizabeth. "In all my years, I have never met such an accomplished woman. She is kind, loyal, intelligent, approachable, and empathetic. Her beauty is unparalleled and, above all women in the Kingdom, she is gracious."

Darcy paused to allow Mr. Collins the opportunity to remember all he said. He waited until the man finished mouthing the words Darcy had just spoken. Finally, the rector spoke.

"You will not marry Miss de Bourgh?"

"I will not."

"You are set on disappointing my patroness?"

"I am."

Mr. Collins shook his head in disbelief. "You will marry this woman then?"

It was an impertinent question that Darcy excused due to the stress of the situation. He could see the gathered perspiration across the man's forehead start to run down the bridge of his nose like rivulets of rain on a window.

Darcy well knew the challenge of trying to change Lady Catherine's mind and envied the clergyman not one bit.

"If I can convince her I am worthy, Mr. Collins." Darcy felt the truth of the statement in his heart. As the months had passed and he witnessed his sister's metamorphosis from a damaged heart to a contented one, his thoughts had regularly drifted to the conversation at the churchyard. Little in his world was kind. He longed to have Elizabeth's companionship and see her smile for the rest of his life.

He would speak no more of Elizabeth to the rector, but his thoughts justified all he said about her. In the two years left until Georgiana's come out for the London season, he needed a woman by his side who would provide tender care and good principles. He wanted Elizabeth.

"Sir! Mr. Darcy, I cannot keep myself from offering the opinion that there is no woman who more qualifies as the 'jewel' of England than Miss Anne de Bourgh. She has all the accomplishments of a woman of elevated rank. Whomever you have chosen must have used her arts and allurements for you to set such a woman as your cousin aside. I beg you rethink your decision for I cannot see Lady Catherine de Bourgh finding agreement with your purpose."

"I am decided." Darcy was ready to end the conversation and get the parson on the road to his aunt's home at Rosings Park. He turned away from Mr. Collins and walked to the window that looked out over the front of the house. "My carriage has arrived and will take you to the north road where you can catch the post coach for Kent.

My driver will wait until you are on your way and will provide the fare so there is no inconvenience to you."

Mr. Collins was confounded. Never had Lady Catherine been as conscious of his personal care. Nevertheless, the rector was unconcerned that Mr. Darcy might be hurt in the process of fulfilling his new mission. He knew in his heart that the superior wisdom of Lady Catherine would prevail. Thus, he vowed to keep any reservations to himself.

"Mr. Darcy," Mr. Collins started the bowing movement he had used when he entered the room. "You are truly a man among men, sir. I will gather my belongings and remove myself from Hertfordshire immediately."

Going to the doorway, Mr. Collins summoned Mr. Hill with demands for speed in packing his trunk. Unbeknownst to the rector, Mr. Darcy had made the same request, though much more calmly done, when he had first arrived at Longbourn. Thus it was only the time it took for Mr. Collins to walk out the door and enter the carriage before he was on his way.

Darcy waited in the opened doorway, wondering when Elizabeth would arrive from her walk. He heard footsteps approaching him from behind. He turned and found Mr. Bennet trying to look around him to see what the disturbance was.

"Pardon me, Mr. Darcy, but I do believe your carriage has departed without you."

Darcy knew men such as Mr. Bennet. They found much

delight in finding humor at the foibles of others. It provided them an elevated view of their own intelligence.

Before Darcy could satisfy Mr. Bennet's curiosity, Elizabeth attempted to walk into the house. The men were still standing in the doorway.

"Mr. Darcy. Papa." Elizabeth curtseyed to both gentlemen.

Darcy had observed her standing at the front corner of the house when Mr. Collins had walked out. He appreciated her wisdom in waiting until the rector was gone.

Both gentlemen stepped back to allow Elizabeth to enter.

"Elizabeth, you walked out this morning?" Mr. Bennet had been waiting in his book room for Mr. Collins to approach him with a request for his second daughter's hand in marriage. Only then would Longbourn be secured for his wife and other daughters should his demise come earlier than he planned.

"Yes, Papa."

"Did you not have an appointment with my cousin?" Yes, Mr. Bennet knew Elizabeth was displeased with the arrangement. However, she was not above her sisters and any other of them, with the possible exception of Lydia, would have accepted their fate with far less rancor than Elizabeth endeavored not to display.

"Yes, Papa." Elizabeth spoke directly to her father. "I noted it was Mr. Collins's habit to rise late of a morning.

With the hour we returned home, I did not expect him to be up and about. Is he, sir?"

"Any why are you here so early young man?" Mr. Bennet had not been notified by Hill that they had visitors. It was an oversight he would not fail to correct.

"Mr. Bennet, I apologize for not seeking you out upon my arrival. It was imperative I come to Longbourn before visiting hours to share some information with Mr. Collins that required his immediate return to my aunt, Lady Catherine de Bourgh. If the matter had not been of a volatile nature which will cause her tremendous consternation, I would not have done so."

"But, sir!" Mr. Bennet was at first furious that his plans had been thwarted, and then pragmatic. Mr. Collins had made his selection from the Bennet daughters and Mr. Bennet had agreed that keeping Elizabeth in his home was preferable to having any other of his daughters in his old age. It was his intention to have Mrs. and Mrs. Collins live at Longbourn after their marriage so that little would change of his daily routine. He expected Elizabeth to keep her husband out of the bookroom. Since he had shared his hopes with his cousin, he was confident Mr. Collins would be back, so confident that he could tolerate a short delay of the betrothal. "Very well, Mr. Darcy."

Mr. Bennet turned away from the couple and left them in the entrance hall.

***

Elizabeth was curious to how events had taken place. She stood her ground when Darcy stepped closer. Keeping his voice soft, he related in detail his conversation with the rector.

"But, Mr. Darcy, sir," Elizabeth was confused. "You did not identify *me* as the woman you chose to pursue. I understood this was your intention."

"You are correct, Miss Elizabeth." Darcy looked into her sparkling eyes as his own softened. "Nonetheless, I could not direct my aunt's ire towards you and your household. It would hardly be fair repayment to have done so. Therefore, I reconsidered my words on my ride to Longbourn after I left you."

Elizabeth pondered the expressions he had used in his description of her. They were lovely words that any intelligent woman with a heart would desire to hear.

Her voice quieted to a whisper. "Did you mean them, sir?"

It was exceedingly bold for her to ask, yet their conversation the night before and earlier that morning allowed them each the freedom to speak what was in their hearts.

***

Darcy noted a curl which had been disturbed when she had removed her bonnet upon entering her home. It bounced next to her head each time she moved. His hand itched to carefully put it back in place. Her face had a healthy glow, her eyes were crystal clear, and her cheeks and mouth were reddened from the cool morning air. She was all that was lovely.

"Yes, Miss Elizabeth, I did."

"Oh!" It was spoken silently, only her mouth forming the words, her eyes widening as she did so.

"Miss Elizabeth, I..." That was as far as he got.

Mrs. Bennet came heedlessly down the stairs, moving rapidly upon them with a screech. The lady was enraged. She marched to the hallway and roughly grabbed her daughter's arm. "I should have known you would run him off. You have no appreciation for my nerves and for the future of your family." She pulled at Elizabeth only to find Mr. Darcy had attached himself to her other arm, holding her in place. "Get upstairs, Lizzy. I will deal with you as you deserve as soon as I see Mr. Darcy out. Now go!"

Elizabeth could not recall ever seeing her mother as livid as she was. Gone was the striking good looks which had originally caught her father's attention. In their place was a face full of fury that pulled her mother's mouth into a straight line and her eyes into narrow slits. She was breathing rapidly and her complexion was the color of boiled beets.

Looking up to Mr. Darcy, Elizabeth calmly asked. "Sir, we shall speak of this at another time?"

"Pray do not ask me not to offer my protection." Darcy gritted his teeth and she could see frustration in the tenseness of his jaw. "It is my duty and honor to see you are well."

She shook her head. "I will be well, Mr. Darcy."

"You are placing me in a difficult position, Miss Elizabeth, one I find untenable."

"I will be well."

Elizabeth knew she left him no recourse and was sad that it had to be so. With resignation, she watched him bow, call for his horse, and walk out the door.

She looked down to where Mrs. Bennet continued to fiercely hold on. Then she looked her mother directly in the eyes. Her mother unwrapped her fingers. Straightening her spine, Elizabeth started to walk to the stairwell, when the front door was thrust back open until the heavy wood portal banged against the interior wall. Turning, she saw Mr. Darcy standing erect and threatening in the doorway. Apparently he had changed his mind.

CHAPTER FIVE

Darcy watched the reactions of the Bennets. Mr. Bennet turned back towards the front of the house and stood next to his wife. Mrs. Bennet spoke not a word, her eyes darting back and forth between both men. Elizabeth walked to his side. The battle lines had been drawn.

"You will not blame Miss Elizabeth for my actions of this morning." Darcy's tone was firm. He had been angered beyond words when Mrs. Bennet had clutched Elizabeth's arm in a manner which would leave bruises on her tender flesh. *No person, not even her mother would be allowed to bring her harm.* "It was at my instigation that Mr. Collins has left for Kent and was a matter which solely concerned him and my aunt. Your daughter was outside the house when I arrived and did not return until after the rector's departure. She bears no guilt."

Mrs. Bennet started to defend her actions of aggression towards her daughter. Darcy held up his palm and turned his head away from her. She received the message. Mr. Darcy would not listen to whatever she intended to say. She closed her lips, irritated that Darcy was having his way in her own home.

"Young man, this is my estate and that is my daughter." The expression on his face indicated Mr. Bennet's displeasure. "You had no right to interfere."

"Mr. Bennet, I am aware I trespassed on your home. However, circumstances demanded immediate action on my part. I have no regrets." Darcy was comfortable in his position of master of his estates and well knew the rights and privileges of being the head of the household. He did not hold Mr. Bennet's statement against him. Nevertheless, the matter of Elizabeth being roughly handled needed addressed.

"Might I inquire, sir, as to why you are allowing your wife to reproach and ill-treat your daughter for something she is not responsible for? Should it not have been my arm Mrs. Bennet grabbed, my person exiled to Netherfield Park, and myself who was threatened with consequences rather than Miss Elizabeth?" Darcy could feel his emotions roiling, threatening to boil up and choke him with their power. He breathed deeply to calm himself.

***

Mr. Bennet looked closely at the young man in front of him and his possessive stance with his daughter. He suddenly saw the ridiculousness of the situation. They were two roosters who were poised to fight over nothing.

Mr. Darcy was correct. He now realized that one situation, the conversation between Darcy and Mr. Collins, had nothing to do with the aborted proposal between the rector and Elizabeth. He dropped his shoulders and exhaled loudly in defeat. Securing Longbourn's future would have to take place another day.

"Mrs. Bennet," her husband gave her his full attention. "It seems we are thwarted in our designs this morning and will need to wait until my cousin's return before our daughter is engaged to be his wife."

When his wife started to speak, he did as Darcy had just done, raised his palm for silence.

"Might I remind you, dear, that Mr. Darcy is a friend and guest of our new neighbor, Mr. Bingley, with whom I understand you hope to attach our eldest. Mightn't this be a fine opportunity to invite the Netherfield party as guests to dinner one evening this week?"

"Mr. Bennet! How you vex my nerves." Elizabeth's mother dug for the handkerchief hidden up her sleeve. "Both Mr. Darcy and Mr. Bingley at my table. I will make sure Jane is at her best."

"Mr. Darcy, should you need to see me, Lizzy knows how to find me. I will, as usual, be ensconced in my lair." Mr. Bennet steered his wife away from the couple and walked back down the hallway. When he got to his study's doorway, he looked back at Darcy and Elizabeth, easily reading their interest in each other, a small smile on his face. Possibly he would not have to have the rector as his son-in-law after all. If Mr. Darcy would secure his family's future, then his cousin would not need to return from Kent. Now he had to figure out how to keep Lizzy without him.

***

Darcy felt like he had been through a whirlwind where he completely lost control. The rapid change in Mr. Bennet's countenance puzzled him exceedingly.

"Elizabeth, might we speak?" As his anger receded, he was unaware of his familiar use of her Christian name. He noted her reaction, her small smile of pleasure. He would not confess to her until years in the future, if even then, that he had silently said her name over and over throughout the night as a chant that brought him peace.

The couple walked into the drawing room, leaving the door wide open. Darcy hoped it would be hours before any of Elizabeth's sisters would travel beyond their bed chambers. Unless her parents showed themselves again, they would be undisturbed.

"Sir, where do you want to begin?" Elizabeth seated herself on one of the chairs close to the fireplace. Darcy sat across from her, though he shifted the chair forward so their conversation would be theirs alone. It was a cozy atmosphere—the snap and crackle of the burning wood a homely sort of sound.

"Your father, Miss Elizabeth, I cannot help but wonder what he is about. He has to know the woman you are—to know you are vibrant and alive, witty and kind. How could a man who loves you not realize what a miserable sort of marriage you would have with a fool such as Mr. Collins? Is your father in ill health? Is there a reason he is, now, afraid for the future of his family?"

"I have spent many hours contemplating these very questions." Elizabeth's sigh echoed from one end of the room to the other. "Mr. Darcy, I inquired of my father why he suddenly made my marriage a priority. His answer was very much a surprise to me." Elizabeth repeated the conversation carefully. "Apparently it was the coming out of my youngest sister, Lydia, which spurred Father to finally give consideration to the future of his five daughters. Since Longbourn is entailed to Mr. Collins, he settled on marriage as the means to keep this estate in the Bennet family. He required his cousin to take on the surname of Bennet so any son produced would continue our father's name. Mr. Collins readily agreed."

"I see." Darcy put his fingers up to his chin as he gave thought to her comments. Unless that agreement was put in a legally binding document, there would be no means of Mr. Bennet enforcing the name change upon Mr. Collins after his death. It could be the end of the male Bennet line.

"Well I am pleased you do so, sir, as I am befuddled by his thinking." The volume of Elizabeth's voice rose. "He has had since Jane's birth twenty-two years past to prepare. As each daughter was born, my father should have felt the weight of responsibility grow to such an extent that he was moved to economize or set aside funds to provide care for not only his daughters, but his wife as well. Papa chose not to do so."

"And your mother?" Darcy had to ask.

"Pshaw!" Darcy could hear the frustration in her voice. "My mother rarely thinks beyond today. It has always been so."

"And, you?"

"Me, Mr. Darcy?" She boldly looked directly into his eyes. "I have begged, pleaded, and cajoled to no success. My comments have surely been as a thorn in the paw of a lion to both parents. I have been speaking into the wind."

Darcy felt her pain and heard her bitterness. One thought kept forcing its way to the surface with each word she uttered. But first, he needed to understand her motives.

"Miss Elizabeth, if you could choose your future, your path, what would it be?"

He wanted to hold his breath. What if she chose to explore opportunities to travel outside of England? He was needed at Pemberley—until Georgiana was happily married and settled, his responsibilities would keep between Derbyshire and London. What if she wanted to learn from the masters, to devote her years to study and attaining learning? She was an intelligent woman. Such a life would leave little time for him. The thought made him unbearably sad.

***

Elizabeth bowed her head to her hands clasped tightly in her lap. She felt a wrestling between her heart and her mind. *Should she open up and express her intimate desires to this man?* A small wedge of concern reminded her that she did not know him well moved into position and threatened to drive her to restrain her tongue. Sighing deeply, she again looked at him, knowing from her innermost emotions how she needed to answer the gentleman seated before her. He had earned her complete honesty by his actions to thwart Mr. Collin's proposal that very morning. It was the least she could do.

"Sir, my desires are not grand, though I believe they are noble," she began. "Yes, the same circumstances which now weigh heavily on my father have long plagued me. Because this is so, I crave security, Mr. Darcy. I desire the companionship of a man who feels that respect and admiration between marriage partners is the most important aspect of a marriage. I yearn for a man who wants to protect me as much as I want to cherish and care for him, a man of integrity and honor. I hunger for a match with someone who would put the needs and happiness of our children ahead of his own life as I would as well." Elizabeth leaned forward, to better capture his attention. She was pleased when he did not look away, not even blinking. "Am I asking too much, Mr. Darcy? Being the daughter of a poor country gentleman, are my standards too high? Is such a man outside my reach?"

***

"Certainly not!" Her words resonated in the deepest

recesses of his lonely heart. Since the death of his father he had not met one woman who had not hungered for his wealth and position in society—until Elizabeth. All the months he had searched for the young woman at the churchyard he had worried that he had built her up to be an unattainable character, that when he at last found her, she would disappoint in the most fundamental qualities he desired in a wife. Instead, the reality was all he could have hoped for—was more than he had hoped for.

Darcy stood and settled on one knee before her, carefully lifting her hands and cradling them in his own. That one thought surfaced and remained. He had to declare himself to the woman before him.

"Miss Elizabeth, I thank you from the bottom of my soul that you did not hold back from telling me what is in your heart." Darcy's deep baritone softened to a whisper, his eyes revealing his feelings more than any words that could be expressed. "My mother and father had a good marriage and I was raised in a happy home. Pemberley was a refuge where I grew up safe in the knowledge that I was loved."

He felt Elizabeth squeeze his hands.

"When we lost my mother, my father lost his way." Pain resonated in his voice. "When my father died, I understood why he reacted as he did. I was bereft." He felt the tightness of her hands grasping his. A tear started from the corner of her eye and moved slowly down her cheek. He longed to move his thumb across the surface to capture that drop of moisture, removing any sadness from the woman in front of him. With surprise, he realized that she was feeling his agony in her own heart and he was feeling a responding depth of emotion. *My pain in her heart and her pain in mine.* That single thought hit him as a lightning bolt from the sky. *Could it be so?*

"Elizabeth, I searched for you. In every town, at every gathering, I longed to find you for I knew in my own heart that you, and only you, could help me mend the broken pieces of my soul so I can be whole again." He heard the soft intake of breath. "I loved the thought of you, Elizabeth. I loved the thought of you with my whole being."

"Mr. Darcy." Without sound, his name slowly came from Elizabeth's mouth.

"Can a heart ache when it is full of joy?" Darcy watched as another tear followed the same trail down the side of her lovely face.

"Yes, Mr. Darcy." He watched warmth fill her eyes until a fire started to burn in them.

"Do you feel my heart, Elizabeth?' Darcy put her hands to his chest. "Do you feel it beat for you?"

Elizabeth swallowed.

With clarity he revealed himself to her.

"I do." Her hand began to softly pat his coat to the rhythm in his chest. "How can this be, Mr. Darcy? We are so newly acquainted." They were valid questions. "Your actions of this morning speak volumes as to your character, yet I do not know you."

"I move too fast." Disappointment filled him. She was right. He was allowing the emotions of the moment to speak for him in a way he had never experienced. *Had it been love at first sight?* It felt real—solid.

"While I know you are a good man who deserves to be highly valued, you have overwhelmed me, Mr. Darcy." She smiled sweetly at the dismay on his face.

Darcy rocked back on his heels, letting go of her hands. She was not rejecting him and for that he was truly grateful. However, her words were like cold water poured over him on a hot day. Had it been a man approaching his sister with such a rush to the altar, he would have castigated him soundly. Elizabeth deserved no less.

"I find myself in unfamiliar territory, Miss Elizabeth." It was Darcy's turn to sigh as he stood. She did as well. "My friend, Mr. Bingley, has the reputation of falling in and out of love quickly. As for myself, I can honestly state that I am, for the first time, understanding what moves him to such tender feelings." He chuckled to himself. "My friends and family would be beyond surprised at me and I admit to being surprised at myself."

"Then perhaps you might accept the invitation to dinner my father was quick to suggest. It will give us opportunity to test these feelings."

"To see if they are real? Lasting?" Though Darcy had no need of more time, he saw that Elizabeth was not as sure that he was the match for her.

"Yes, Mr. Darcy." Elizabeth tilted her head, raised her brow, and smiled. He saw the mischief and squared his shoulders, preparing himself for her volley, unknowingly smiling in return. "I feel it is only fair for you to see me at my most frazzled. Yes, dinner at Longbourn should do."

He wanted to gather her into his arms and promise her the world. However, it was not the world she wanted, only his presence at dinner. That he could and would do.

CHAPTER SIX

"Mr. Darcy, how may I be of service?"

Teetering stacks of books covered every surface of Mr. Bennet's study, threatening to distract Darcy from his purpose. A desire to create order out of chaos sprang up in his chest to the point that he found himself reaching for the closest pile before he stopped himself. He doubted Elizabeth's father would appreciate his assistance.

"I am come to accept your invitation to dinner on behalf of myself and the Bingley family, sir." Darcy remained standing as he had not yet been invited to be seated. Mr. Bennet had not even offered him the courtesy of rising when he had entered the room. This lack of proper manners did not bode well for the conversation, Darcy suspected.

"I judge you are a young man used to having your way." Confidence oozed from Mr. Bennet. "I am Oxford educated with an extensive background in the study of characters, Mr. Darcy. I also have the benefit gained from decades more of life's experiences." He looked the man over. "I am certain my wife will be glad of your acceptance, Mr. Darcy."

The tone was dismissive and Darcy could not keep the flash of ire from his eyes.

"Are you a lover of the game?" Darcy pointed to a chess board positioned on a small table under a window. There appeared no dust so it had recently been used.

"I am. You, Mr. Darcy?"

Darcy could hear the condescension in the older man's voice. He sensed the attitude of superiority in both Mr. Bennet's countenance and his tone. Darcy had spent his lifetime in company with such men. They lived on small estates yet felt they were a vassal king to a miniature kingdom, subservient solely to England's throne. They hid under their ownership, begging for protection, though they did nothing for themselves and those under their care.

"I played many a time with my father." He carefully worded his comment. He would give nothing away to his opponent. "It has been some years since I have done so." He mentioned nothing of the many matches he played since his father's death.

"Then let us have a game." Enthusiasm and victory dripped from Mr. Bennet, as if he had already won the match.

Darcy knew the routine. The board was utilitarian and well-used. As it stood, the black king rested on its side — checkmate. It did not surprise him at all to have Mr. Bennet sit on the side with the white pieces, without words indicating he had been the victor of the prior game. The player with the white pieces always moved first.

The board was reset, the pieces put in place and Mr. Bennet made his first move. As Darcy moved his hand over the pawn, Mr. Bennet spoke.

"I surmise you find enjoyment in my daughter's company."

Withdrawing his hand before touching the piece, Darcy looked at the man closely. Mr. Bennet had not looked up from his perusal of the board, as if he cared not for Darcy's response. Nonetheless, the hand resting on the table was tightly fisted. Mr. Bennet cared.

"I believe you would be surprised if I did not." This was a familiar game — verbal thrust and parry. Since his youth Darcy had practiced fencing with the masters. His father taught him the power of using words wisely. "I also do not doubt that one of your greatest pleasures is spending time in conversation with Miss Elizabeth."

Elizabeth's father snorted, yet said nothing. He waited until Darcy made his first move and lunged. A bold move much different to a skilled parry.

"What are your intentions towards my daughter?"

The corner of Darcy's mouth lifted. "She will be my wife." It was plainly said.

"Humph!" Mr. Bennet refused to glance at his opponent. "You do not know her well enough, Mr. Darcy, to make such a determination. My Lizzy is a simple girl who has not been raised to manage an estate. She has no skills outside of a minimal interest in music, which she plays poorly. Find a woman in your own sphere. Leave my daughter to me."

Anger surged in Darcy's chest. *How dare a father speak in such a way of a daughter he should love and cherish.* "I believe Miss Elizabeth would be both surprised and distressed to hear herself described in such a way by you."

Again, Mr. Bennet snorted. He said nothing in reply as the game continued in silence.

Darcy realized that Elizabeth's father had every intention of walking away with both his pride in his chess skills intact and a confidence that his daughter would remain in his home.

"You insult the child who has striven the hardest to gain your approval." Darcy again acted with hesitancy in making his next move, though his voice was firm. "And these are the actions of a good father?"

"I know what you rich men are about, Mr. Darcy. You see young girls like my daughter as a way to pass your time and ease your boredom in the country. When you return to London, you will forget about her as she is left behind with her heart broken and crushed." Mr. Bennet's bishop slid across the board, it's opponent seemingly vulnerable.

Darcy could see that the older man wanted to rub his hands together, but did not so nothing was given away.

"You do not know me enough to accuse me of such, Mr. Bennet." Darcy had his own strategy for the game. He also had his own path for the conversation. "I became acquainted with Miss Elizabeth in July of this year, sir. This is not the work of a moment."

"July, you say." For the first time, outright disdain covered Mr. Bennet's face. "I have heard nothing from her about you, Mr. Darcy. You must not have made much of an impression on my impressionable child."

Another piece moved across the board.

"Your *child* was mired in a pit of despair at your plans for her." Darcy hesitated over his move, as if unsure. "How could you do that to her?"

"You have no right to question my parental decisions. It is I who knows what is best for Lizzy."

"No, sir." Darcy countered. "You only know what is best for you."

"And where is the error in that, young man?"

Darcy's play seemed haphazard and ill-timed, as if he barely knew the rules of the game and was guessing at the movements of each particular piece.

"Miss Elizabeth shared that you did not involve yourself in the lives of your children until your youngest came out in society." An advance. "That this same event happened to coincide with the request of your cousin for a bride must have seemed felicitous to you."

"It was." A retreat.

"I cannot imagine Miss Elizabeth not being clear in her opinions of marriage to Mr. Collins. You have to know she is miserable at the thought."

"She will be content to be mistress of Longbourn."

"Will she, now?" At this there was a change of engagement, a move to give a swordsman an advantage or to play their target as a fool. "How long would she have to live with your cousin under your roof before that event would take place? Decades? A quarter century or longer?"

"I am ready to end this game and this conversation." Thomas Bennet smirked. "I would like to offer a wager, Mr. Darcy." He stared his opponent in the face. "I propose we make the results of this game more interesting."

Darcy wanted to smile. He did not. He had been a master chess player at Cambridge. He supposed Mr. Bennet had been the same during his university years, though the intervening decades would have likely provided no real challenge for him from the residents of the neighborhood. He imagined Elizabeth's father had taught her the game enough to stimulate competition, though not to win. At least he hoped so.

It was twenty minutes later when Darcy walked into the drawing room. His eyes found his target. Elizabeth was seated near the window, ignored needlework resting on her lap. Mrs. Bennet and the remainder of her daughters were either engaged in sorting ribbons or looking at fashion plates in well-used women's magazines.

At his entrance and rapid approach, Elizabeth set the embroidery hoop aside and stood.

There was no preamble, only a direct approach. "Miss Elizabeth Bennet, would you do me the honor of accepting my hand in marriage?" Darcy's words were clipped, his voice easily carried across the room.

***

Elizabeth heard the screech of her mother and the squeals from her youngest sisters. She ignored them and peered into Darcy's eyes.

"You are angry, sir." She could see the muscles of his jaw clinching as his teeth almost ground together. He did not even look at her while he made his brief proposal.

"I am."

"May we walk in the garden so I can provide you an answer there?" Elizabeth tilted her head and looked even closer at him. Even under distress, he truly was the handsomest man she had ever seen. However, having her younger sisters and mother as witnesses would not do.

"You are not rejecting me, then?"

"I am not." Elizabeth quickly responded, surprised how sensitive she was to his regard. "Nor am I accepting you...yet." In a move meant to calm the situation, she touched the back of his hand where it was fisted at his side. The pain that had flashed in his eyes at the thought of being rejected had touched her heart. *Why did she feel his hurt so deeply?* "Sir, might we speak of this privately?"

"No, Elizabeth!" Mrs. Bennet interrupted. "You will speak of it here. But I caution you, girl. Before you answer you need to consider the future of your sisters, not just your own. Mr. Collins has made promises for the family consistent with his positon as cousin. This man," she waved her hand at Darcy, "with his ten-thousand a year is far more suited to a beauty like my Jane. Jane could not be so beautiful for nothing. Mr. Bingley's five-thousand a year will not do! I will see that Mr. Bingley is for Mary. I will have three daughters married!"

***

Darcy saw the flush cover Elizabeth's face at the vulgar interference of her mother. He knew he would hide nothing from her. When she heard of what her father had done, she would be even more appalled. It certainly was in his favor for her to know as it would almost guarantee her acquiescence. Nonetheless, he wanted her willing agreement to his proposal, responding from desire rather than distress.

"Mr. Darcy," Elizabeth whispered so only he could hear. "Are you, indeed, set on this course?"

"I am." He moved his other hand to cover hers.

***

"Why, sir?" Before he had gone into her father's study, he had been close to declaring himself. She had been close to accepting him. Nevertheless, reason intruded. Elizabeth needed to be sure of her own heart and of his. Time needed to be allowed to do so. But something had happened with her father. She could still feel his ire radiating from him until it surrounded her. Elizabeth worried over what had taken place between the two men.

"Will you trust me, Elizabeth?"

She hesitated before she replied. In truth, they knew each other so little. Yet what she did know about him harmonized with her own desires. He was tender towards his younger sister and careful with his guardianship. He had been willing to overlook the faults of her family in his pursuit of her. There was nothing else to be done. "I will, Mr. Darcy."

"Will you call me Fitzwilliam?"

"As you have called me Elizabeth?" She smiled and her eyes softened.

He smiled in return. "Yes." He whispered.

"You have struck a bargain with my father, then?" The idea was repugnant to Elizabeth.

"You are too quick."

Taking in a deep breath and letting it out slowly, Elizabeth clasped both his hands in hers, squeezing tightly. She could not move her eyes from his.

"Yes, Mr. Darcy, I will marry you. I will be your wife." This was stated so all in the room could hear. She wanted her mother to know there was no hesitation on her part.

Surely Darcy's exhale could be heard inside the house. "You will be mine."

Ignored were the noises from the other Bennet females. Neither Darcy nor Elizabeth were aware her father was standing at the doorway until he uttered, "Oh, Lord. What have I done?" When they both looked towards him, it was to see his retreating form as he headed back to his bookroom.

CHAPTER SEVEN

"I pray you, Fitzwilliam. Tell me what happened between you and my father." Elizabeth sat on the cold stone of a garden bench. They were far enough away from the house to be undisturbed, though anyone looking outside the drawing room window could see them. Currently, there were three female faces pressed against the glass: Mrs. Bennet, Kitty, and Lydia.

"I do not know how, Elizabeth." Darcy dropped his head to his chest, shaking it slowly back and forth. "It will cause you pain."

This was the moment that had filled Darcy with dread since he left the bookroom. He reached over and took Elizabeth's gloved hand in his. Then he rethought his actions, removing both his glove and hers before entwining his long fingers with hers. He needed the touch and it seemed to provide her comfort as well.

"Fitzwilliam, I will not give you an argument or challenge your right to keep information from me." He looked up at that. "But please know that my imagination is vivid. For example, I imagine from the manner in which you came into the room and proposed, my father wagered my future; a wager you must have won." When he started to shake his head in the negative, she continued. "You were unhappy and angry when you offered for me, sir. Your sense of honor had to have been battered by whatever happened in my father's study. Am I correct?"

Again, Darcy contemplated her mental agility. He was pleased it was most likely superior to his own.

"Yes, and no, Elizabeth." A sigh ripped from Darcy's chest. "You are both correct in your conclusion and entirely wrong."

***

She pondered what he meant. Then she truly looked at him. He was not withholding information because he did not believe she was undeserving or unable to understand. He was protecting her. His very nature had to be screaming at him to remain silent so she would never know the depths her father had plunged to in his quest to secure his family.

"Oh! No! No! No!" Elizabeth put her free hand to her mouth. "It was not just me, was it? It was not only my future my father bartered with. It was my mother and my sisters as well." She saw the truth on his face. He could hide nothing from her. "What was the wager, Fitzwilliam?"

Darcy cleared his throat.

"We played chess." At Elizabeth's nod, he proceeded. "Our discussion was becoming heated when he challenged me. If we were at cards, he would have increased the stakes of the game. As it was, he decided that the winner of the match would receive the desire of his heart. The deal he offered was that if he won, I would leave Hertfordshire and never see you again. You would marry Mr. Collins and live the rest of your life at Longbourn. If I won the game, I would have full financial care of your mother and sisters—and you."

Embarrassment flooded Elizabeth. She was ashamed of her father for the first time in her memory. Once Fitzwilliam was engaged in the game, his honor would not allow him to back down. It appeared to her that whichever way the game might have gone; Darcy would have lost.

"I am so sorry. So very, very sorry." Tears streamed down Elizabeth's face so that she failed to see Darcy's puzzled expression.

"Elizabeth. Elizabeth!" He cupped her cheek, raising her face until he could see her eyes. They were in agony. "I did not lose. I won."

"I am aware you won the game, sir."

"Not just the game, Elizabeth, I won it all." She finally noted his joy. It was then Elizabeth understood that his sadness was for the hurt in her heart, not his. "Do you not see? I won the right to marry you. I won the right to settle dowries on your sisters. I won the right to educate Kitty and Lydia—Mary as well, should it be her desire. I won the right to see your mother settled comfortably in Hertfordshire, amongst her peers, for the remainder of her life. All of this will ease the mind of the one woman whom I will cherish for my lifetime. To me? It is worth every shilling, every single one."

"So my father abdicates control and gains what he longs for most; to be left undisturbed in his bookroom." The thought frustrated Elizabeth greatly.

"No…" The corner of Darcy's mouth lifted in a crooked adorable smile. "I would say the punishment will be all his."

"How is this possible?"

***

He could stand no more. Darcy wrapped his arms around her and pulled her to his chest. He delighted at how invincible it made him feel.

"I pray you are satisfied with my plan." He squeezed a bit tighter as his smile grew exponentially. "You see, when Bingley came to Hertfordshire, he not only surveyed the estate of Netherfield Park, he looked at Purvis Lodge, Hay-Park, Ashworth, and Stoke. I shall purchase one of the estates and see your mother and sisters settled there upon the future demise of your father. However, I believe the portion of my plans which will become your father's biggest regret will take place when my aunt, Lady Catherine shows up in Hertfordshire."

Elizabeth tilted her head to the side and raised her brow. "What are you thinking, sir?" Her voice was stern.

"I may not know your family well, my dear, but I do know my aunt. When she finds out I will be marrying a relative of Mr. Collins, the man will no longer possess the living at Hunsford. My aunt will see to that."

"But, sir. Once a living is given, it cannot be taken away." Elizabeth's confusion was easy to see. Darcy understood. The law was the law.

"This would be so if you were anyone other than Lady Catherine de Bourgh. She has long marched to her own tune, making and breaking laws at her whim. Because she is a force of nature in her own right, few have made the effort to correct her. It is why I have had such a time convincing her I will not marry my cousin. She simply refuses to listen."

"How will this affect my father?"

"I have no doubts Mr. Collins will accompany my aunt. When he no longer has a position, I will merely remind Mr. Bennet of his offer to house his cousin until the time the estate passes to him. Whether or not Mr. Collins takes the name of Bennet or not, he will live at Longbourn. I cannot see there ever being peace and quiet for your father."

A chuckle burst from Elizabeth. "Nor will he remain undisturbed." Her smile beamed forth. "You are a wicked man, Mr. Darcy."

"A wicked man, Elizabeth? Surely not!" Warmth filled his chest where the lonely hole he had carried so long had been. Lord, but she delighted him!

"As you were strong and wise for me on this day, Fitzwilliam, I will be your rock when Lady Catherine and Mr. Collins comes. Together we will be formidable."

Darcy was overwhelmed. Never had he thought he would find such a woman, nor that she would be his own. He could not wait to marry her and take her to London. It was an easy step to envision days and weeks spent with his wife and his sister. Days filled with intelligent conversation and kind attention. He sighed aloud. *His wife!*

"What are you thinking, Fitzwilliam? You have the most beatific smile on your handsome face." Elizabeth leaned her face into the hand he still held there. He responded by rubbing his thumb across her cheek.

"I am thinking of the fundamental difference between your father and me. Where he has viewed the future of his family with regret and shame for his inattention, I look to our future with pleasure. Each time Georgiana and I spoke of you, which was quite often, she would always express a desire for me to find you so you could become the best of friends. Now you will be sisters. I could not be happier, Elizabeth."

"Then I am pleased for both of us, sir." Elizabeth paused. "Do you not worry that this is taking place so rapidly?"

"I do not!" His voice held no hesitation. "For, think, Elizabeth. In the two days I have been in your presence, we have quickly learned to express ourselves honestly and without fear. I know few marriages where the partners do so, even marriages of many decades. How can we not do well with such a magnificent start?"

"Your point is well made, Fitzwilliam." She smiled up at him. "I have told you things I have never shared with Jane, and we are the closest of sisters."

That made him proud and he could feel his chest swell at the thought.

"Yes, dear Elizabeth, this is fast, but I believe we are both committed to the happiness of the other. How can we fail?"

"Love never fails." Elizabeth whispered of one of Mary's favorite Biblical texts. It was a universal truth; something reliable and unmoving.

She did not know she had said it aloud until he asked her, "Do you love me, Elizabeth?"

She hesitated before she answered. "I will reply honestly, Fitzwilliam. I have never felt these emotions in my lifetime."

"What emotions?" He had to know.

"Tenderness, Fitzwilliam." Her eyes…those sparkling, vibrant orbs glistened with emotion. "My heart is full of such sweetness and my soul yearns to cherish you in the same way you have done for me. Whether it is love or not, dear man, we have laid a foundation of stone which we can build upon."

Darcy nodded. It was enough. "My father told me many times that the day he and my mother wed, he thought he could not possibly feel more love for a woman than he did at that moment. Then he would laugh at what he thought was true love as each passing hour brought a depth, height, and width he never knew existed. When my mother died, he told me that *then* he knew love."

"What a lovely story. I will treasure those words in my heart." She moved even closer to him. "Do you not believe in your soul that we will do the same?"

"I do." Instinctively, Darcy started swaying back and forth, rocking her in his arms. He thought back on his youth. "I cannot say their marriage was without discord as I remember many times they disagreed on subjects small and large."

"I believe we will do the same." She sighed into his coat.

"I do as well, dear woman." He smiled into her hair. "And I hope we resolve these differences the exact same way."

"Oh, how is that?" Elizabeth pulled back to look him in the eye. "You have stirred my curiosity and it demands satisfaction."

"With a kiss."

"Oh!" Elizabeth mouthed the word.

It was temptation incarnate. Her lips were rosy and full. He could not help but gather her closer, lowering his head a fraction.

"May I kiss you?" It came out a whisper.

"Yes, Mr. Darcy. I wish you would."

And he did.

CHAPTER EIGHT

When Elizabeth's mind cleared of its passionate haze, she realized that, against the chill in the autumn air, Darcy's lips were incredibly warm—and soft—and firm. And they deliciously fit hers perfectly. She wanted to sigh or swoon—or perhaps, both.

She had no will to look away from him. His eyes revealed all his emotions and were filled with the pleasure of their agreement and their kiss. She loved his smile, which currently covered his face. Apparently he loved her kiss as well. She could not help but smile in return.

Eventually, Elizabeth became aware of tapping on the large drawing room window, which sounded like loud explosions in the walled garden.

Both her and Darcy turned their heads to look at the house as Mrs. Bennet's squeals accompanied Lydia's staccato beats on the pane. Their intimate moment had been interrupted.

As they walked closer to Longbourn, they easily discerned the activity inside.

"I want someone to kiss me like that, Mama." Lydia bellowed into the glass, her forehead bumping the pane for emphasis. "I want him to be rich and tall; an officer with yellow hair and blue eyes. A handsome man who adores me and loves to dance." The youngest Bennet continued voicing her opinions. "Lord, how ashamed I would be if I was not kissed like that before I was Lizzy's age."

"I want an officer too." Added Kitty into the fray, only her voice was muffled as she was not so close to the glass. It came out sounding like, 'I want an off tooth', which was ridiculous.

"Girls! Girls!" Mrs. Bennet insisted on having her say. Her voice was so loud she was easily heard outside the house. Now that Elizabeth would not be marrying Mr. Collins when he returned from Kent, Mrs. Bennet sought to benefit her family by this union and match him with her middle daughter. "I cannot imagine what Mr. Darcy sees in her. I would think it better if Jane was to be his wife and mistress of his large estate. Nevertheless, once Lizzy is married, she can invite you to Mr. Darcy's house in town to put you in the way of other rich men. Mr. Collins can have Mary."

Pangs of embarrassment shot through Elizabeth at the unrestrained conduct of her sisters and mother. She watched as Kitty and Lydia joined hands and jumped around the room, proclaiming in a sing-song voice about all the balls and parties they would be attending.

Mary was heard denying all desire to marry the rector, her countenance bordering on the comical. Elizabeth had witnessed her middle sister practicing such a pose in the mirror. When asked, Mary said she felt it was a pose which she felt gave added credence to her proverbial sayings. Elizabeth thought she looked pious and silly both then and now.

Elizabeth could look no longer and secretly wished herself and Darcy a million miles away.

"My dearest Elizabeth, do not be distressed." Darcy squeezed the hand he was still holding. "I am marrying you, not your family." He paused in thought. "I do believe it would be prudent to rethink my plan."

Panic filled her chest. "You do not want to marry me?"

"Of course I will marry you." Darcy hurried to reassure her. "What I will not do is reward bad behavior. I can overlook insult to myself and to my property. What I will not condone are any slights to you or to Georgiana, not even from those related to us. Your mother's words of surprise that I would marry you instead of Miss Bennet anger me beyond measure."

"What will you do, Fitzwilliam?" They had reached the front of her home. She stopped walking and faced him.

"My first response when I won the privilege of caring for you, was to set your mother up in a style superior to what she had known in her marriage so her husband, your own father, would feel the burden of failure." He acknowledged Elizabeth's indrawn breath with a nod. "Yes, dear one, in many ways your father has failed."

"I pray you do not do this, Fitzwilliam, for it would be an unnecessary expense and a lesson wasted on him." She was learning more with each passing minute about both men. One was honorable and unselfish, while the other had only the appearance of it.

"My belief is the same, Elizabeth." He gave her hand a gentle squeeze. "Therefore, I will not purchase an estate for Mrs. Bennet. Instead, I will look for a small, well-kept cottage in Meryton, possibly close to Mrs. Phillips. It will be large enough to house all of your sisters, if they are still at home when your father passes away, but small enough to match her thinking towards her second daughter, who, though she is not her mother's favorite, is most assuredly mine."

The muscles in Elizabeth's cheeks were starting to burn from the width of her smile. "Then you believe I deserve a larger home?"

Darcy laughed aloud, his rich baritone ringing through the countryside.

Elizabeth was mesmerized and knew in her heart she could listen to that particular sound for the rest of her life. She would make it a matter of priority to coerce him to repeat the same every day of their marriage. A worthy goal.

"What I believe, my dear, is that Pemberley was made for you; that past generations cultivated and planted solely for your enjoyment."

How could she not rejoice at such a comment?

"I spent the remainder of the night after the Meryton assembly with my imagination on fire, vividly picturing you in our homes brimming with happy children and love. I even had chuckled so loudly at one point when I considered how unlike myself I was being that it disturbed my valet—and I rejoiced in it, though Parker, my servant for the past twelve years, did not."

"You silly man!" Immediately her mind imagined the same. "Your words bring me peace. A gift most unexpected."

"Your family, my dearest, will need to earn the privilege of visiting you. If they cannot or will not recognize your true value, I will not tolerate their company." He paused in reflection. "I thought of lessons I had learned from Mrs. Northam which apply to our situation. 'Treat others as you expect to be treated.' It was Norty's version of the Golden Rule. We will have peace, my lady."

Elizabeth thought on his comments and relished his firm commitment to a successful marriage. If only her father would...no, Elizabeth would not go there. She would be leaving Longbourn. Her home was with Darcy.

"Possibly *after* Lady Catherine has come and gone from Hertfordshire?" Elizabeth could not help but tease.

The exhale coming from Darcy caused his shoulders to drop. Then he squared them in determination. Not even his aunt would rob him of contentment. He would simply not allow it to be so.

"Yes, Elizabeth, only then." He wrapped her in his embrace.

"I must be off."

Elizabeth was loath to see him go. However, he had spent so little time at Netherfield Park with his friends that he needed to attend to them, and she knew this. Charles Bingley's invitation had been, in part, to be in company again with his friend, but the main thrust of the invite was to beg Darcy's help with oversight of the estate. While he had been raised to care for the responsibilities of landownership, Bingley had not. Yet Darcy had spent the majority of his time in her company instead. She was not complaining.

The groom patiently stood with Darcy's horse as the couple moved closer. Elizabeth's discomfort was not solely with his departure. She had been young when she had last ridden and fallen off a horse, now preferring her own legs to the four.

"Elizabeth Bennet. While I deeply appreciate you feeling the loss of my company, I am thinking this is not the sole reason your steps have slowed almost to a halt." He asked.

"You do not ride?"

"Not if possible, sir." The response was rapid and clipped.

"So you *can* ride. You just do not *like* to ride? Is it their height which is bothersome?"

Elizabeth's laugh had an edge to it.

"My dear man, it is not that they are so tall, for I dearly enjoy being in the topmost portion of the highest oaks." She swung her arm in an arch encompassing the nearby forest. Then she dropped her chin and looked up at him, her eyes luminescent. "It is that they refuse to stand in one place. A horse moves randomly and rapidly from side to side. I know better to climb a tree when the wind is strong and does the same. Why should I try to sit on the back of an animal who clearly does not want me there as it irritatingly steps wherever it wants?"

***

It was a charming mental picture, though he sensed that a smile or chuckle at her expressions would not be welcomed. He was learning to read her and he thrilled at the thought. Darcy and Georgiana both enjoyed riding the fields and trails of their Derbyshire home. He hoped to share all his daily activities with the woman standing alongside him.

Much had been accomplished since the night before. He had arrived in Hertfordshire as a single man with a large fortune searching for the only woman with whom he wanted to spend time. He had found her in Elizabeth. Now he was returning to Netherfield Park less than four and twenty hours later as an engaged man. Darcy could not be happier.

"Upon my word, Mr. Darcy. Whatever are you thinking?"

"Why?" he challenged.

"We were speaking of horses, yet your face beams with joy, my dear man." She caressed his cheek lovingly. "Your sister would wonder if she saw you at this moment who this happy man was wearing her brother's clothing."

He stepped closer.

"Elizabeth." He whispered on a breath as he lowered his lips to hers. She melted into his arms and his heart pounded so loudly he feared they could hear it over the three miles to Netherfield Park.

When had he become so tactile? He could not seem to keep the grin off his face and concluded that if he continued, he would gain the reputation of smiling too much. *Good! Competition for Bingley and Jane.*

Finally, breaking away and stepping back, he mounted the horse and stared intently at the woman below him. She was glorious and his heart filled at knowing she would be his.

"I will see you tomorrow, Elizabeth." His voice was deep with purpose.

"And I will be looking for you, Fitzwilliam."

With one last glance, he turned and rode away.

***

Elizabeth stood watching him as he took gentle command of the horse. It was a telling move that was one more piece of knowledge to add to those she had learned over the past day. She was surprised when he stopped the horse and rode quickly back.

As he got closer, he slipped his boots out of the irons, grabbed a handful of mane with his left hand, swung his right leg over, and dismounted before the horse had come to a complete stop. Once off, he dropped the reins to the ground next to where Elizabeth stood, pulled her into his arms, and kissed her with a thoroughness she did not know was possible. By the time he finished, they were both out of breath. He moved his face back to see her eyes. She could still feel his exhalation on her cheek.

"I will write to my man of business tonight, Elizabeth, so we will have a special license and the marriage settlement within a se'nnight. Marry me then?"

She heard his unspoken plea and inherently knew how to respond.

"Will you kiss me as passionately after we wed, Mr. Darcy?" Elizabeth's eyes twinkled in delight.

"Much more so, my darling almost-wife."

"Then, yes, Mr. Darcy. I will marry you in one week's time."

He flashed a smile before kissing her again. Then he leapt on his horse and rode off without once looking back.

Elizabeth put her hands to her lips and shook her head. *How could a woman be so pleased?* Freedom from the threat of Mr. Collins had emboldened her. Where she had looked with dread on the marriage to the rector, she looked with joy at marriage to the man from Derbyshire.

Once Darcy was out of sight, Elizabeth turned and entered her home. Only one week more would she be a resident. One week. The thought surprised her in that she felt no sadness. For a certainty, she would miss her family. In spite of their flaws, she loved them all. Yes, she loved her father as well. Without him she would not have life. Therefore, she would be no man's wife and Darcy would continue in his lonely state. Had her father not allowed her to travel to Derbyshire with the Gardiners to come to terms with her future, she would not have met the Darcys. And had he not made such a foolish wager, she would not know the peace of having her mother and sisters settled while her own years would be spent with a man she could lo...lo...love? She was in *love* with Fitzwilliam Darcy? What a perfect realization!

CHAPTER NINE

"What were you thinking, Papa?"

"About what subject, daughter?" Elizabeth's father despised confrontation.

"Papa, I feel like I've experienced the full range of human emotion in the past four and twenty hours. I will have no peace until I understand why you gambled with our future in such a cavalier manner." Elizabeth swallowed. "It is most unlike you."

Mr. Thomas Bennet had known from the instant Darcy had laid his opponent's king over on its side that this confrontation with his daughter was inevitable. *What could he say?* He had felt the heavy guilt resting on his shoulders, though in the intervening hours since the game, he had been able to shrug the majority of it off. It was his way.

"Lizzy, do you like your young man?" He thought to distract her by changing the subject.

"I do." was her immediate answer. She was not distracted.

"Then whatever I was thinking matters not, does it?" He excused his lackadaisical conduct in one question though it bothered him to lose the admiration of his favorite daughter.

He could see the struggle to contain her sarcasm written clearly on his daughter's face. Even though he had raised her to laugh at the follies of others, he would not have appreciated her doing so to him.

"Has he shared with you his plans for our family?" Mr. Bennet had been confident that the only salvation for his wife and daughters lay with Mr. Collins. To have both his plans and his self-proclaimed superior intellect challenged and won by a much younger man was humiliating. His instinct was to look upon Darcy with disfavor. Nevertheless, Elizabeth desired him over Mr. Collins, not that Mr. Bennet was much surprised.

"He has." Mr. Bennet knew if he dug in his heels in the matter of stubbornness, she would dig deeper.

Though he longed to know what Darcy had in store for his remaining daughters and his wife, Mr. Bennet would not lower himself to ask. Instead, he raised his brow, something which had always drawn a response from this particular child. This time it was to no effect. Finally, he stood from his bookroom chair and walked around his desk to where Elizabeth stood.

"I have been a selfish being all my life, Lizzy, in practice, though not in principle," her father began. "As a child I was taught what was right, but I was not taught to correct my temper. I was given good principles, but left to follow them with the laxity I chose. Unfortunately, as the eldest child and only son I was spoilt by my parents, who, though good themselves, allowed, encouraged, almost taught me to be selfish and lackadaisical; to care for none beyond myself." He reached out to take her hand.

"Lizzy, I will not ask for your forgiveness as I am well aware that I am undeserving of such. Note, I pray you, that it was within my rights as your father to arrange a marriage. The mere fact that it is called a marriage of "convenience" suggests the wedding would be of benefit to both partners or their families." He took in a deep breath. "I will, however, do what I can to ease your way."

***

By this point Elizabeth was no longer surprised when he slipped some justification into his conversation. It added to her disenchantment.

"Papa, until this summer when you decided to engage me to your cousin, I would have said that next to Jane, I knew you and felt closer to you than any other person in the world." Elizabeth's eyes were dry and her voice was steady. "Nevertheless, your abdicating your responsibility for our family's care, your dropping that heavy weight on my small shoulders without any consideration for my future happiness, was a disappointment I will carry with me for a time—a long time."

Her father stepped back, though he continued to hold onto her hand.

"Yes, I am now promised in marriage to a wonderful man who will make changes to this household which will guarantee good outcomes for my sisters. If you truly mean what you say, that you will 'ease my way', then I ask you, no, I beg you, to restrain Mama and my youngest sisters tomorrow when the Netherfield Party arrives. Though we are used to their outbursts and Mama's nerves, others are offended by them. Should Jane have any hope of becoming attached to a gentleman such as Mr. Bingley, there can be no embarrassment generated by Mama, Kitty, or Lydia."

Mr. Bennet used his free hand to rub over his face. Elizabeth knew he would consider this request a hardship. His pattern was to ignore a situation until it either resolved itself or disappeared. She waited for him to reply. Finally, he did so.

"I will speak to your mother." He breathed in deeply.

When he offered no more, Elizabeth raised her own brow in imitation of him, placing her free hand on her hip.

"And I will confine Kitty and Lydia upstairs." For the first time since Elizabeth's birth, she did not try to pacify him or make things easier.

Mr. Bennet dropped his chin to his chest and then looked back at the clearness of her eyes, the lift of her chin, and the erectness of her spine. "You have grown up, my Lizzy."

"Thank you, Papa." As if she were already the mistress of a large home, she turned and walked out of his bookroom.

***

"Mr. Darcy, wherever have you been? We have seen little of you since your arrival."

In Darcy's opinion, Caroline Bingley would have been a pretty sort of woman if she had learned to modulate her tone and the critical words which spewed from her mouth with regularity. She was well-dressed and trained to care for a home. Her dowry was twenty thousand pounds and she should have appealed to Darcy. She did not.

"Am I to report my comings and goings to you, Miss Bingley?" Darcy's happiness did not overshadow her impertinence at asking such a question and the sternness of his voice indicated he was displeased. It was not her right to know his business. However, had Elizabeth asked him the same? Darcy smiled at the thought. He would have answered her readily.

"I beg your pardon, sir." Caroline swallowed and looked closer at Darcy. "Mr. Darcy, are you well? The smile on your face...well, your expression is puzzling. It is not a look we have seen in your company."

"I rejoice to see it. Darcy can be quite a dour creature when he is not occupied." Charles Bingley walked to greet his friend and stand by his sister. "I am pleased you are returned, Darcy. I was planning an afternoon visit with the Bennet family and wondered if you wanted to travel with me?" Bingley waited, his posture one of impatience and anticipation.

"That would work well for me, Bingley. It is proper to get to know the neighborhood. Your house is the most important in Hertfordshire and your position is one of which your neighbors would welcome." He changed the subject abruptly. "By the by, we are invited to dine at Longbourn tomorrow. I took it upon myself to accept for all." At that, Darcy bowed to the room and left to wash and change his clothing, the smile still on his face.

Bingley's grin showed a row of straight white teeth. "I suspected Darcy had already been in Miss Elizabeth's company this morning and Darcy, with the invitation, just confirmed my supposition."

"Oh, Charles, you think you know everything." Caroline Bingley stood with her hands on her hips, her foot tapping on the marble floor. "If we are to be in company with these chits, it is time to go through my closet so the Bennet females will know what a woman of elevated rank looks like." She huffed as she walked away.

"It is good to have a goal, Caroline." He said to her retreating back.

**

The evening started well. Caroline Bingley had been ready on time and the five of them fit in Darcy's carriage without her and her sister's dresses and hair being squashed—a vital concern to a well-coifed unmarried woman. They were welcomed to Longbourn with the fanfare deserving of having company above their sphere in the household. Caroline lapped it up like a thirsty puppy.

Charles Bingley immediately went to Jane Bennet's side while Darcy headed to Elizabeth's. Bingley's sister and her husband, Mr. and Mrs. Hurst, spoke with Mrs. Bennet while the three youngest Bennet sisters sat quietly in a corner.

Apparently Mr. Bennet had spoken firmly with his wife and two youngest as Darcy noticed their conduct was vastly improved. At the insistence of his wife, Kitty and Lydia were allowed downstairs with the adults. It was a battle Mr. Bennet felt he would have lost, so he surrendered. So far they had caused no harm.

When dinner was announced, Darcy was pleased to offer his arm to his betrothed. Bingley did the same to Jane and Caroline. Caroline had jockeyed into position where she assumed Darcy would escort her to dinner and her ire was piqued when he did not.

Without Kitty and Lydia's giggles and loud chatter and Mrs. Bennet's nervous outbursts, the only noise around the table was the quiet whispers between Darcy and Elizabeth and Bingley and Jane. Gratefully, Mrs. Bennet had allowed open seating so they were able to choose their dinner companion. Caroline Bingley was not at all pleased.

Thus it was a surprise, either unpleasant or delightful, depending on the hearer, to most of the guests when Mr. Bennet stood to make an announcement.

"Yesterday morning our daughter, Elizabeth, accepted an offer of marriage from Mr. Darcy. I have given my blessing and consent."

The uproar was instantaneous. Mrs. Bennet had been prepared for the announcement and had resolved to maintain her composure, but failed in the end. Caroline Bingley had shouted, "No!" into the fray and Bingley had jumped up to offer his congratulations.

Nobody in the dining room heard the carriage arrive. None heard the thump of the heavy wooden cane on the marble entrance hall floor, and not one person realized Lady Catherine de Bourgh and Mr. Collins were standing in the doorway—until she spoke.

***

"Fitzwilliam Darcy!" She had entered the room with an air more than usually ungracious. The expression on her face proclaimed her desire to be anywhere other than at Longbourn. She had been forced to travel an inconveniently long distance in the company of her insipid rector and she was determined to use everything within her power to halt her nephew from making a terrible mistake. Lady Catherine de Bourgh wanted heads to roll.

Her rector followed her into the room, though he stopped a step behind her, as if seeking refuge from an oncoming threat.

"Lady Catherine, I expected your arrival, though hoped it would have been at Netherfield Park to save Elizabeth from this confrontation." Darcy looked down at Elizabeth as she lifted her chin to him and smiled. "I will not tolerate poor manners in front of my betrothed."

"Betrothed!" Both his aunt and her rector spoke at the same time.

"Yes, Lady Catherine." He did not address Mr. Collins. "I have offered my hand to Miss Elizabeth Bennet and she has accepted. We shall be married."

"This is not to be borne." Fury poured from his aunt like water from an overflowing dam. "Since infancy you have been destined to marry Anne. You are meant for each other." She stepped closer, her chin lifted, and her eyes direct. "You do not intimidate me, Darcy. I have known you since you were in leading strings. Your family will be displeased that you have shunned your responsibilities, that you will bring shame to Pemberley and the name of Darcy, and that you are forsaking proper guardianship of Georgiana by attaching yourself to this woman of decidedly inferior birth."

"I think not, Lady Catherine. So many times I have heard the same rant from you that I almost know what you would say before you utter it. I am in no way terrified by you." He smiled in the face of her rage. "I shall have such causes for happiness that I can, on the whole, have no cause to repine."

"You obstinate, headstrong boy! I am ashamed of you! Is this your gratitude for the guidance I have provided since the death of your dear mother, my own sister? Have you no consideration for the loss both Anne and I will suffer at being abandoned for a young woman who is so far below us? Who is her mother? Who are her family?" Lady Catherine stepped forward, her finger shaking at her nephew. Mr. Collins paced himself so he remained just behind her. "I am no stranger to the machinations of a girl who wants to use you to reach the first circles of society where we reside. She has used her arts and allurements and you have foolishly been blinded by your own desires."

Lydia gave a most unladylike snort. "Arts and allurements? Lizzy? Well, it is blatantly obvious you do not know who you are talking about. My sister would not know an allurement if it hit her in the face. What a joke!"

Caroline Bingley used the distraction to stand and move next to Lady Catherine's side.

Lady Catherine caught the movement and demanded, "Who are you and what are you about?"

Caroline had not imagined she would be so addressed.

"I am Miss Caroline Bingley. I, too noticed Miss Elizabeth using her flirtatious ways with Mr. Darcy at the assembly in Meryton only two nights past. I stand beside you, Lady

Catherine."

"You? A Bingley?" Lady Catherine gave a sound very similar to Lydia's, though she would not call it such as a woman of her sphere simply did not snort. "Does not your family reek of trade? You seek to attach yourself to my nephew? Never will that happen. Now, sit back down. You are not wanted or needed here."

***

At that, Elizabeth stood and clasped her hand into Darcys. He did not know if she needed support or was wanting to give it. It mattered not.

"That is enough!" Darcy moved away from the table, drawing Elizabeth to his side. They were a team — comrades in arms. Again, he looked at Elizabeth and smiled. Then he looked back at his aunt, his eyes piercing into hers. "You have no right to enter this home. You have no right to advise me. You have no right to declare me as engaged to Anne, and you have no right to expect me to follow your commands. For five years I have been my own master. For five years you begged for assistance rather than offered help when I desperately needed it after father died. I have been alone, Lady Catherine. Once I marry Elizabeth, I will have a home filled with love and joy. We will guide Georgiana to a marriage which will be full of the same. I will be wed to a woman I love, admire, and respect. I will no longer be alone."

His words met with silence, until Mr. Collins spoke.

"Pardon me, Mr. Darcy. I am exceedingly sorry to inform

you, the nephew of my most noble patroness, that you cannot marry Miss Elizabeth."

"I cannot? Why ever not?" Darcy was not in the mood to be addressed by the rector. William Collins was not a threat to him now nor would he ever be.

"Because she is betrothed to me."

Lady Catherine spun on her heels at his words. "This is the girl you were planning to bring to Hunsford? Miss Elizabeth Bennet? You shall receive the full force of my fury for doing so."

"Yes? No?" His voice stuttered. "But for you, Lady Catherine, I will end the engagement with Miss Elizabeth and marry one of the other Bennet daughters." He bowed so low he threatened to tip over.

"You imbecile! I am done with you. Return to Kent and pack your bags—immediately!" Lady Catherine dismissed him with no concern for the law or the fact that the night was already dark. "You may make your home in this squalid cottage. I have no use for you anymore."

Before Lady Catherine could turn back to Darcy, the Reverend William Collins, approached Mr. Bennet seeking refuge for the night and a home as soon as he returned from Hunsford Parsonage.

That arrangement appeared satisfactory to Mrs. Bennet. She was no different than the mothers of the ton. A single man who would inherit an estate, even if it was her own, was highly desirable.

"I shall have a room prepared for you right away, Mr. Collins." Mrs. Bennet rubbed her hands together in pleasure. She turned to her second daughter. "I can almost forgive you for putting me through this ordeal, Lizzy."

Again, Darcy spoke up to regain charge, only to have Elizabeth's free hand rest on his arm. It stopped him, his attention redirected from Lady Catherine to his betrothed.

"Fitzwilliam, did I hear you correctly when you stated that our home would be filled with love and joy?" Her eyes were luminous when she looked up at him. "Were your words spoken with deliberation?"

Darcy patted the hand on his arm.

"They were." He grinned at her, his eyes soft and warm.

"I see." Her smile grew to match his; her voice was a whisper. "Are you saying, then, that you love me as I do you?"

So focused were they on each other that they became unaware there were others in the room.

"You love me?" Darcy was stunned. He had never thought to hear the words so soon.

He saw the twinkle, then he looked at her lips to her smile. It was brilliant.

"You want to marry me then? Really want to?" His heart had to be sure.

"Yes, Mr. Darcy."

What else was there for him to do? In front of the Bingleys, the Hursts, the Bennets, his aunt, and Mr. Collins, he lowered his head to hers and kissed her firmly on the lips. She kissed him back.

"Well I never!" Lady Catherine's pitch resembled Mrs. Bennets when she was intensely frazzled. "I am deeply offended at your conduct. That my own nephew would do something so improper, so against the rules of decorum and propriety, in company with heathen tradespeople in a house which one day would belong to Mr. Collins is against everything I know. Honour, decorum, prudence, nay, interest, forbade it. I am leaving, Fitzwilliam Darcy. You will rue the day you stood against me."

The great lady turned to walk out. ``I take no leave of you, Darcy. You deserve no such attention. I am most seriously displeased.''

"Are you seriously displeased?" Darcy whispered to Elizabeth as he finally drew his head back from hers, completely ignoring his aunt.

"Not at all, Fitzwilliam. There is nothing that pleases me more than to be in your arms." She snuggled closer. "Are you?"

"Never!" Darcy kissed her again briefly. "Do you not

know that Mr. and Mrs. Darcy shall be reported to be ridiculously happy by all and sundry? We shall live a long life together and scoff at those who say we were not meant for each other. Are you agreed?"

"Oh, yes, Mr. Darcy."

He still held her to his chest when Lady Catherine stomped out the door.

CHAPTER TEN

At the same time Mr. Bennet loudly cleared his throat, Kitty coughed, Mary preached the sins of anger, corruption, and lust, Caroline Bingley squealed in anguish, Mrs. Bennet's mouth hung open, Mr. Collins gaped at the couple, and the Hursts, Bingley, and Jane smiled with shared happiness for Darcy and Elizabeth. Not one person remaining in the dining room mourned the loss of Lady Catherine's company. She would have felt the lack most acutely.

"Oh Lord, Lizzy!" Lydia had stood from the table and was now walking in a slow circle around the couple. "I hope to never marry a short man. Look how your head fits perfectly under his chin." She stopped and put her finger to her cheek, tilting her head. "I thought I wanted someone similar to John Lucas, but I do not believe his arms are long enough to wrap me as tightly as you are being held." The youngest Bennet looked up and caught Darcy's eyes. "I would not have thought it, Mr. Darcy, but you will do for Lizzy after all."

Darcy realized Elizabeth had long ago learned to overlook her youngest sister's strongly expressed youthful opinions. For him, it was a relatively new experience. He could feel the heat in his face and knew the tops of his ears would be bright red. Yet he counted the cost of a temporary embarrassment against having Elizabeth in his embrace and knew he would put up with anything to keep her there.

"I commend you for your keen observation, Miss Lydia." What else could he possibly have said to an impertinent young girl who should not have been at the table?

"Me too, Mr. Darcy." Kitty chimed in. "I want to marry a tall man too."

Darcy finally stepped away from Elizabeth and bowed to the second youngest. "I shall keep that in mind, Miss Catherine."

"Mr. Darcy, you have sullied my sister's reputation by your ungentlemanlike conduct." Mary's spectacles perched at the end of her nose and her chin was raised while her head turned slightly to the side. "In spite of the fact that Mr. Collins intended to offer for her sooner, you shall have to marry Lizzy. It is the Christian thing to do."

"Thank you, Miss Mary." For the life of him, he could think of nothing else to add.

"Well, Mr. Darcy, it seems you must, indeed, marry my Lizzy. My children and wife have spoken." Mr. Bennet seemed resigned. "The events of the evening will provide fodder for years of entertainment and though I do not want to lose Elizabeth, I now know I am doing so to a worthy man."

Darcy noted Elizabeth's embarrassment as her eyes went to her eldest sister. Jane's head was bent as a rose blush covered the parts of her face that he could see and her hands twisted and pulled at the napkin in her lap. He felt their mortification.

"I am sorry." She mouthed, for his eyes alone. "That such a great man would choose to overlook the impropriety of my family eases me, Fitzwilliam."

"I am sorry as well, Elizabeth." Darcy had been appalled at his aunt's conduct and the vitriol spewing from her mouth. If anyone should be ashamed of their relatives, it would be him. Nonetheless, there was no reason to accept blame for the bad behavior of others.

"Fitzwilliam, I believe that what tests us will make us stronger."

He took her small hand in his and could not keep the smile off his face. It continued to amaze him how comfortable and at peace he felt in her company. *Had it only been three days since he spied her at the assembly?* So much had happened, it was difficult to imagine so few hours had passed.

"I say, Darcy," Bingley stood and spoke. "My family and I join in extending hearty congratulations at your betrothal. You are the most fortunate of men to have captured a woman who makes you happy. I hope each and every day draws you closer as your family grows and flourishes." He lifted his glass. "May you have grey hair that comes from old age, wisdom, and worry."

At that Darcy cocked his head, lifting his brow in the process. Elizabeth looked first at Bingley and then back to Darcy. Mass confusion filled the room. Only Caroline Bingley spoke.

"Whatever do you mean, Charles? Mr. Darcy is possessed of a fine home, wealth, a good name, and the highest position in society." Caroline stopped and pressed her hand to her forehead. "Oh, I catch your meaning. It will be upon his marriage to Eliza Bennet that he will have reason to worry. Yes, Charles, very well said."

"Caroline!" Disapprobation radiated from Bingley as he spoke sternly to his sister. "You misunderstand me."

He turned his back to her and looked at his friend. "Darcy, I have watched you worry and fret over your sister these past five years. Actually, I have watched you worry and fret over just about every matter under the sun." He stopped at the chuckles from the others in the room. "The worry I wish you will come when your first girl child is born. If she looks like her mother, you will love her with such passion that your hair will streak with silver as she nears the age to come out and marry. Your firstborn son will add to it by riding his pony at breakneck speed over the fields of your estate. He will swim before you are ready and run when you wish him to walk. You will plan and organize and plan some more when your second son is born, then your third and beyond…only to have them independently strike out on their own. Oh yes, Darcy. You will worry; but you would have it no other way."

"Thank you, Charles." Darcy was almost overcome with emotion. "We will remember your words always." He raised Elizabeth's hand to his lips and kissed the inside of her wrist. He caught the glint of tears at the corners of her eyes and knew that her heart, too, had been touched.

The rest of the evening was spent in pleasant discussion, at least for Darcy and Elizabeth. As the Netherfield party filed out of Longbourn for the return trip to Bingley's estate, Darcy walked alongside his betrothed.

"We weathered our first storm, Elizabeth."

'That we did." Elizabeth squeezed his arm. "And we are still engaged to be married."

"That we are." His gazed down at her with such depth of feeling that his chest felt like it would burst. He stopped walking before they reached the carriage. The moon was waning and Elizabeth's lovely face was bathed in the moonlight.

"Elizabeth, do you recall your words to Georgiana the day you spoke to her in Lambton?"

"I do not, Fitzwilliam." It had been almost three months. She remembered the occasion and her impressions of the two, but not the spoken words.

"You asked Georgiana what Norty would say if she was still here; what lessons she would have learned from the circumstance she mentioned to you at the graveside."

"Oh yes, I do recall now."

"My dearest, loveliest Elizabeth. If Mrs. Northam was here next to me, she would ask me what I now know that I did not earlier."

"And what have you learned, Fitzwilliam?"

He reached his free hand up and touched her cheek. "All of those months I searched for you, I loved you. I loved your kindness in speaking to a lonely, confused girl who was wholly unrelated to you. I loved the tenderness in your heart to have approached her and your care in dignifying her feelings. I loved your firmness in not allowing her to excuse her own decisions."

Darcy was overwhelmed at all that had transpired with his sister. "Elizabeth, people in my world do not treat others in such a fashion. I learned then that if I ever found you, I would need to be a better man. I would need to be the best man I could be."

"Fitzwilliam, you are the best of men. I know it to be true." She quickly reassured him.

"And I learned what my father meant when he thought he loved my mother to the fullest on his wedding day, only to find out what true love was as they met the daily challenges and joys. For I love you so much more at this minute than I thought humanly possible. I look forward to whatever tomorrow brings as I will end the day loving you more than at the start."

"Oh, Fitzwilliam. I will hold these words in my heart for as long as I live."

"Do you love me, Elizabeth? Really and truly love me?"

He could not wait for her answer. His heart demanded action, so he kissed her with a passion he did not know he possessed. She answered equally and he could hardly breathe with the emotion.

"Do I love you, Fitzwilliam? Does my heart rejoice at the thought of what tomorrow will bring? Do I look forward to a future at your side?" Elizabeth leaned her cheek into his hand. "Do you fill my heart with joy? Have you come to mean the world to me?"

She paused, taking in a deep breath.

"Yes, Mr. Darcy. A resounding 'yes' to all." She stood on her toes and kissed the corner of his mouth.

He kissed her then with such feeling that he missed the collective sigh from those outside.

"You will marry me?" One last reassurance.

"Yes, Mr. Darcy."

EPILOGUE

Ten Years Later

The hallways of Pemberley resonated with the sounds of happy children. The Darcys' five boys were joined by Charles and Jane Bingley's three daughters. Mary Bennet, who had never wed nor had never
been inclined to do so, was trying to herd them outside into the garden without damage to the valuables in the niches along the corridor.

Mrs. Hurst was heavy with child, so their family remained at their townhouse in London, as it was too dangerous for Louisa to travel this close to her confinement. Miss Bingley, had foolishly entrusted her dowry to the treacherous Mr. Wickham, the same man who had tried to elope with Georgiana all those years ago. He had presented himself to Caroline as a close friend of the Darcys. In a short period of time she was penniless. Thus, Caroline was forced to remain with the Hursts to care for the two young girls in the household as she no longer had an income of her own. She had never been able to move past the jealousy she felt towards Mrs. Darcy so had not, until George Wickham, accepted the attentions of any other gentlemen. Afterwards, Hurst and Bingley refused to sponsor her in society. For her, it was the bitterest of blows.

Georgiana Darcy was thrilled when her brother wrote to her that he had found the young woman from the cemetery. When he mentioned his betrothal to her in the same letter, she had been overjoyed. Elizabeth Darcy had become a trusted friend and confidant. When Georgiana had met and fallen in love with Lord Winters, the Marquess of Devondale, it had relieved her heart to have Elizabeth ease her brother's way.

Elizabeth watched the children and her sister from the stone bench in the center of the garden. Her husband soon joined her.

"Did Jane bring news of the rest of your family?" Darcy had come to dread the annual visits of Mrs. Bennet. Both Kitty and Lydia had calmed with the discipline of the headmistress at their finishing school. Kitty had married an injured soldier living in London who took up the law. Lydia had fallen head-over-heels in love with the new rector of the Meryton parish. Therefore, she lived but a short distance from her former home.

Elizabeth chuckled softly. "According to my eldest sister, who has never said an unkind word about anyone, Papa and Mr. Collins have become combatants in their own home with Mama in the middle. Jane called her the mediator, but I cannot see it."

Darcy sniggered. "I can see in my mind's eye your father

using his intellectual prowess to keep Mr. Collins from his bookroom. I can also see Mr. Collins being entirely unaware of these efforts and bursting into where he is most unwelcome, completely oblivious to his being uninvited, offering to share his spiritual counsel and wisdom with your father."

The mental picture was a comedy of errors. Over the intervening years, Elizabeth was able to carry on conversations with her father, but the relationship never returned to the days prior to the summer Mr. and Mrs. Darcy met. She had come to terms with this soon after she married Darcy. She had her own family and her own home.

"Jane also told me that Mama would be tending Lydia during her confinement."

Darcy snorted loudly, a most ungentlemanly sound.

"I cannot imagine your youngest sister being any happier this time than she was when her son was born." He squeezed his wife's hand and asked, "What was it she told your mother?"

A laugh burst from Elizabeth. Certainly her mother would have found no humor in the conversation, but it was classic Lydia.

"She informed Mama, in no uncertain terms, that if she needed no assistance to become with child, she needed no help delivering it."

Darcy's head nodded up and down at the memory. "Yet, your mother is not here?"

"No, she is not." Elizabeth shook her head, her eyes closing. "According to Mama's last letter, even though Lydia has been married to a responsible man these five years, she is her baby and needs her mother."

Both Darcy and Elizabeth sighed, pleased that Mrs. Bennet did not live close. Since Mary had moved to Pemberley less than a year after the Darcy marriage and the Bingleys had moved from Netherfield Park to Derbyshire that same year, the only Bennet child remaining in Hertfordshire was Lydia. Mother and daughter butted heads regularly with neither willing to give in. It had to be difficult for Lydia's husband, at least Darcy presumed so, yet the man loved his wife fiercely.

As Darcy loved his wife. He looked at the children to see if any were watching before gathering Elizabeth in his arms. For some reason, his older sons delighted in teasing him about displaying affections so openly.

"Will Anne come to Pemberley, dearest?" Elizabeth had been sad for her husband when his aunt had succumbed to a cold. Lady Catherine had insisted that people did not die from a trifling sniffle, yet she had done so. Darcy had so few family members remaining that the loss of even one as cantankerous as Lady Catherine was missed.

"I expect her later today."

"And your Fitzwilliam cousins?" Lord and Lady Matlock rarely left London, but both their sons were country born and bred. The Fitzwilliam boys loved to tease Darcy as he was the youngest male cousin. Both men had made arranged marriages and both men had girl children. The abundance of Darcy males had been a source of continuing irritation as there needed to be an heir born to inherit the earldom.

"Elizabeth, dear. Are you prepared for all this company?"

"You know I am, darling." Mrs. Reynolds, Pemberley's housekeeper, ran a tight ship and the house was ready for the influx. "I am hopeful this child will not be born while they are here. It would not dare. Too much noise will fill our home and I am afraid our babe would enter the world only to want to return to the quiet comfort of my womb."

Darcy gently rubbed the large bump hiding his wife's abdomen.

"Do you long for a girl, Lizzy?" Her husband had long ago shorted her name when his emotions were engaged.

"I long for a healthy child, Fitzwilliam." She had suspected her husband wanted a daughter, especially since Georgiana married. He loved each of his sons from the fullness of his heart, but a daughter would be a precious gift to him.

"As do I, Elizabeth." He sighed. "But to have a little girl with her mama's beautiful eyes and curls to hold in my arms would be a pleasure. I will not deny it."

"Then we will hope for a girl."

They smiled at each other as she leaned into his side.

"Elizabeth, are you happy with our life? Is our marriage what you had hoped it would be?" Even he heard the uncertainty in his voice.

"You are a silly man!" Elizabeth leaned up and kissed him. "I love you, dearest, with my whole heart and soul, so, yes, Mr. Darcy, I am happy I am your wife."

He held her close and surveyed his home, his land, and his family. Of all he possessed, of all he held dear, it was Elizabeth Darcy who captured his heart.

"You love me, truly?" He needed to hear the words.

As Elizabeth opened her mouth to answer, she felt the baby roll from one side to the other as another dull pain throbbed in her lower back. Grabbing her husband's hand, she laid it over her extended waistline so he would feel it as well. A smile lit his face and his eyes sparkled with delight.

"Truly, absolutely, positively I love you." She returned his smile, hugging him as closely as she was able. "You may ask me a million times a day and I will always answer the same. Yes, Mr. Darcy, I love you."

Darcy recalled the day just over a decade before when he had searched for his sister. Then he remembered the diligence he showed in trying to find Elizabeth. He smiled into her curls, kissing Elizabeth on the forehead without being aware he had done so. His life and the life of his sister had been bleak until a ray of sunshine had walked into the cemetery.

The promise he had spoken to Elizabeth when Lady Catherine had confronted them at Longbourn, that they would be happy as Mr. and Mrs. Darcy had come true. He was a happy man.

Children's laugher drifted to where the couple sat, bits and pieces of the conversation standing out from the others.

"Ewwww! Uncle Darcy is kissing Aunt Lizzy again." Bingley's eldest, six-year-old Sarah, was as precocious as Elizabeth had been. She turned her nose up and twisted her face to show her disgust.

"Ah, do not worry, Sarah," the heir to Pemberley responded. "It is a sight we often see so we rarely give it any notice."

"Let us play lord of the manor, William." Bingley's second daughter asked. While Sarah loved the outdoors, Emily gave all her attention to her dolls. She was a quiet girl who, at five-years of age, was in training to become an excellent wife.

"Oh, please, no. Let us not." Nine-year-old William Darcy did not want to play with girls. Nevertheless, he knew his parents would be displeased if he did not. The Bingleys were guests in his home and he knew his responsibilities.

He sighed deeply so that both Darcy and Elizabeth heard him.

"Very well, Emily. I am the master. Will you be mistress or will Sarah?"

Emily Bingley had a very clear sense of what should take place in a home.

As the children's voices moved away, Elizabeth clasped Darcy's hand firmly in her own, her breathing shallow and her face pale.

"Oh, Fitzwilliam. I am afraid I may have misjudged who might be the next arrival to Pemberley." The grip on his hand increased to an intense pressure.

"Is it time, Lizzy?" He was going to become a father again. Joy filled him from his head to his toes.

She looked at him with love in her eyes.

"Yes, Mr. Darcy."

Almost The End

From the Author: If you would like to find out if they had a boy or a girl, please turn the page. If not, thank you for reading my story. I hope you enjoyed it.

POST SCRIPT

The elderly man paused before walking into Darcy's study. With the birth of this child the Darcy's lives would forever change. He took a deep breath and tapped on the door.

***

Darcy had been fretful. In every way this birth was different from the others. Few minutes had passed between the start of Elizabeth's pains until her waters broke. The last five times his wife had given birth she had remained calm, at least in his presence. It had not been the case this time. He knew Elizabeth through and through. The rapidity of the birth process had her worried. That alone made him frantic.

Had the babe come too soon? Were his wife and child in danger? In every way the thought terrified him. He prayed. He supplicated. He begged for protection for his family and promised himself he would leave Elizabeth alone from this day forward so that she was never with child again. Then he recalled doing the same during each of the five prior births. Darcy sighed so deeply it rattled his chest. He would not leave her alone.

"Enter!" The doctor had come. He would learn his fate.

"My wife, is she well?" Darcy could not even wait for the man to sit.

"For a certainty, sir, be assured that Mrs. Darcy is in excellent health."

"The babe?"

"Also in good health though she seemed quite perturbed at having her life changed so dramatically." The doctor had served the Darcys for decades. He had watched the Master of Pemberley grow from his childhood into an honorable man who cherished his family and protected all under his care. Thus, he was overjoyed to share his news.

"She?" Darcy whispered as if he was hesitant he had heard incorrectly. "I have a daughter?"

"You do, Mr. Darcy."

***

Before he could finish, the younger man had vacated the room and rushed upstairs. The doctor imagined the new Miss Darcy would have her father under her control as quick as a breath. He smiled. "Oh yes, Mr. Darcy, your life and the lives of your sons will forever change. Little girls have special powers when it comes to a father like you."

The doctor allowed himself the opportunity to rest in one of the study's comfortable chairs and pondered how long it would be until Mrs. Darcy was increasing again, because he was confident the lady could only ever respond in one way to her husband. "Yes, Mr. Darcy."

The End

ABOUT THE AUTHOR

Joy Dawn King started telling stories from an early age. However, she did not write any of them down until she was 57 years old. While living high in the Andes Mountains of Ecuador with her husband and family, she read Jane Austen's Pride and Prejudice for the first time. It was love at first page. After she was done, she longed for more.

When searching for another copy of Jane Austen's writings, she happened upon several books that offered alternative paths to happily ever after for Mr. Darcy and Elizabeth Bennet. She purchased and read as many as she could find. Finally, in early 2014, she had an idea for a story about the couple that would not go away. Thus, her first book, A Father's Sins: A Pride and Prejudice Variation, was born.

Since then, Joy and her husband moved back to the U.S. and plot bunnies kept hopping in and out of her imagination. Now, it's all she can do to keep up with them. But, she tries.

BONUS PREVIEW – THE ABOMINABLE MR. DARCY
(to be published Summer 2016)

Oh! That abominable Mr. Darcy!"
—Jane Austen, *Pride & Prejudice*

CHAPTER ONE

Wednesday, 2 October, 1811
Meryton, Hertfordshire

He was by far the handsomest man she had ever seen—tall and broad-shouldered with dark wavy hair, curls flirting at the back of his collar, and sapphire eyes that sparkled in the myriads of candles lighting the assembly. Elizabeth Bennet, like the others in attendance, watched his progress as his party entered the room. His clothes were of the finest materials and the fit was excellent. She wondered if he was a fastidious man. He looked the part.

Elizabeth glanced to her sister Jane to determine where her eyes rested. *The red-haired gentleman. Good!* She loved her sister dearly. If Jane was interested in the taller man—who the whispers of the assembly determined was Mr. Fitzwilliam Darcy of Pemberley in Derbyshire—Elizabeth would gaze at him no more. Since this was not the case, her eyes again drifted his way as the group walked through the crowd.

Besides *Mr. Divinely Attractive* and the red-haired man, two other men and two women accompanied the party. It was simple to surmise one of the pairs was married by their deliberate movements to ignore each other.

"Eliza, I believe you will have to restrain your two youngest siblings when they spy the officer's red coat." Charlotte Lucas, who was seated on the other side of Elizabeth, had a practical mind. They were long-time friends in spite of the seven-year difference in age. She too was surreptitiously studying the newcomers. Any unmarried man would be ideal prey for the abundance of maidens in attendance, herself included.

Elizabeth's eyes alighted to the officer behind *Mr. Heavenly Visage.* He had a pleasant, welcoming smile with a touch of the sardonic. Like *Mr. Stately Sculpted,* his brow was furrowed. Elizabeth could not help but wonder if he had seen action on the continent. The colonel was ruggedly handsome with bronzed skin, indicating many hours spent out of doors. He was not as tall as *Mr. Overtly Gorgeous,* yet the shoulders of his uniform were just as broad. Neither man looked as if they needed padding to enhance their physique. Elizabeth watched his easy smile as his eyebrows rose at something *Mr. Sublimely Appealing* said. She immediately judged him as a man whom she might find much delight in knowing. *Was he a second son to have chosen the military as a career?*

"Yes, Charlotte, I believe you are correct," she said sighing. Her younger sisters, Kitty and Lydia, were uncontrolled and ill-mannered, far too young to be out in public. Nonetheless, their mother insisted they be let loose at age fifteen to hunt down and capture a husband. The girls had long been fond of a man in uniform.

Elizabeth turned to look closely at her friend, only to find Charlotte's eyes lingering on the colonel. She smiled to herself. *It was as she had hoped! No interest in Mr. Fabulous.* Sweeping her eyes around the room, she spied Charlotte's father headed in their direction, most likely to retrieve his daughter for an introduction to the new arrivals.

"I believe you are about to be summoned, Charlotte. Now, as Mama would say, 'Stand up straight with your shoulders back.'" Both young women chuckled. Yet, both knew with clarity why their mothers acted so. Only if their daughters married or sought work as a governess or companion would their families be relieved of their support.

As her friend walked away, Elizabeth again looked around the room. It was an interesting drama that was unfolding. The set had ended so the noise had diminished as the dancing couples moved to find refreshment or their next partner. Voices carried across the room.

"Come, Kitty and Lydia. Jane, smile, he's looking your way. Mary, oh where is that Mary?" said a flustered and frantic Mrs. Bennet. "Lizzy can meet them later. Girls! Come! Our neighbors from Netherfield Park have arrived. Come!"

"The lack of fashion and good taste is appalling," said the young lady in the puce dress to the woman who was endeavoring to keep up with her. "How could Charles possibly want to settle in Hertfordshire? There is no one here of quality who would not be a hardship to be in company with."

"Unless our brother and his friends stand up with us, I fear I shall not dance this evening as Gilbert has gone to the card room. I shall not be able to roust him out." The speaker had features similar enough to the young woman in puce and the red-headed man to identify them as siblings. *They must be the Bingleys.*

Elizabeth watched as Sir William Lucas, accompanied by his wife, two daughters, including Charlotte, and their two sons, approached the Netherfield party; his voice booming to the far corners of the assembly hall.

"Mr. Bingley, might I introduce you to my family?"

As he brought forward his wife and children, Elizabeth spied her mother herding four of her daughters to a spot behind Sir William, a position where she would be noticed. Elizabeth slunk back into her seat, wishing she was in any other location to avoid witnessing her mother's antics to promote her own daughters to the gentlemen. Furthermore, she detected regret on the faces of Mrs. Long and Mrs. Goulding that they might have been outmaneuvered.

As Elizabeth anticipated, both of Mr. Bingley's sisters acknowledged the Lucas and Bennet ladies with barely a slight nod and then looked away with practiced ennui. In fact, the two were twittering behind their fans. Elizabeth's ire grew as she saw the embarrassed blush creeping up her eldest sister's neck at the supercilious sisters' slight. Jane Bennet was above reproach and therefore was, in Elizabeth's opinion, entirely undeserving of their condescension.

Elizabeth's anger was lessened as she realised Mr. Bingley's attention was solely for Jane. The taller man? *Mr. Sublimely Appealing* looked straight ahead to the opposite wall, giving a slight bow once all the individuals had been presented. *Was he above the present company? Was he shy? Perhaps he is mute or he has difficulty with his tongue? A stutter, maybe?* He was an interesting riddle to be puzzled out in her own mind.

Once the social niceties were concluded, Mr. Bingley led Jane to the dance floor as the colonel did the same with Charlotte. Conversation flowed between the latter couple, while the former gazed at each other with infant feelings of admiration.

Before Elizabeth could return her own gaze to the handsome gentleman, she heard her mother's voice with a dread that made her quiver.

"Mr. Darcy, I have another daughter who is not presently dancing. I am sure you would not neglect the young ladies who are without a partner?"

Sure enough, Elizabeth realised Kitty and Lydia had been claimed for the next set and her quiet sister Mary had returned to her book on a bench in the corner. Her mother had turned and was pointing in her direction, wagging her handkerchief at her. Elizabeth was seated with three other young women who had not been claimed by a dancing partner for the current set. She felt the heat as her face flushed. *Why? Oh, why does my mother have to embarrass me so?* Possibly the man would not realise which of the four ladies Mrs. Bennet was attempting to draw his attention to.

She could only hope.

Elizabeth glanced up at the gentleman and gratefully realised his eyes had not moved from the point he had been focused on since he had entered the room. Curious to determine what had captured his interest, she looked behind. *Bare panels of wood!* There was not even an unusual knot or burl in the planking to attract the eye.

Elizabeth knew in her gut that his reaction to the matriarch of the Bennet family would be telling as to the type of man he was. Therefore, when he offered her mother another bow and walked away without saying a word, Elizabeth realized he had been repulsed by her mother's blatant attempt to coerce him to favour one of her daughters. From Elizabeth's vantage point, it was not a flaw. Even she knew her mother's conduct had been vulgar.

Elizabeth suspected what was coming as if she had written a script for their actions. As soon as *Mr. Practically Perfect* decamped, Miss Bingley followed. Where she went, her married sister followed; two shadows attempting to move in harmony with the reality.

As Elizabeth turned her attention back to the dance, she heard Charlotte's laughter and realised the colonel was exactly as she expected him to be—pleasant company. Mr. Bingley's grin radiated satisfaction with his partner, and Jane's cheeks were pink with joy, not embarrassment. They made a lovely pair, all smiles and blushes. Watching them made Elizabeth smile as well.

Elizabeth had no way of knowing how the candlelight danced in her eyes as she found pleasure in the interest Mr. Bingley was showing her sister. However, Mr. Darcy noticed. To him, she was a mystery, and he wondered which family she belonged to. He appreciated that she was seated regally, as if overseeing her little kingdom. Rich golden highlights danced in her dark hair from the chandelier above, leaving her in a pool of brilliance — as if the heavens were nodding their approval.

Darcy drew in a breath, considering how his attention had been caught so quickly by a country miss. Yet he assured himself he would soon discover her to be as inane and superficial as almost every other unmarried young woman he met — more concerned for his estate and his family name than himself. The company he had met so far gave credence to his thoughts.

When the dance ended, both Mr. Bingley and the colonel escorted their ladies to where Elizabeth was seated. She stood at their approach and curtsied deeply as Charlotte and Jane introduced the gentlemen.

"Miss Elizabeth, if you are available for the next set it would be an honour for me to stand up with you." Upon closer inspection, the colonel was older than she had first presumed, or his experiences in the military had prematurely caused lines around his eyes and mouth. Elizabeth was determined to find out.

When the music started, it was a slow country dance where they would be able to converse during much of the set. Elizabeth smiled in delight at the realization.

She had no clue she was being observed.

"Miss Elizabeth, you were not with your sisters when we were first introduced. You have yet to meet my cousin." Colonel Richard Fitzwilliam often took it upon himself to nudge Darcy into being more sociable. Though the two men were intimates, the nature of the both gentlemen were complete opposite in manners.

"The tall man with the quizzical brow?" Elizabeth's own eyebrow lifted as she spoke, her eyes twinkled and a grin appeared.

The colonel chuckled. Here was a young woman not intimidated by his cousin's stern manner. "Is that how you would describe Darcy?"

"It is all I know of him."

"You have heard no rumours of his wealth? His status?" Even he had been confronted with the loud whispers of "ten thousand a year with a large estate and a house in town."

"For a certainty, Colonel Fitzwilliam, I have heard what my neighbors are saying." Elizabeth paused as they moved away from each other in the dance. "Yet, wealth stays with us a little moment if at all. Only our characters are steadfast, not our gold."

"Sophocles?" He was caught in surprise at the slip of a lady in front of him. No other woman of his acquaintance could quote ancient writers.

"Euripides."

"Ah, the great playwright from ancient Greece." They both laughed as both authors were ancient and Greek. In a blink, the colonel's countenance changed from jovial to one of earnestness. "Nonetheless, my cousin is the finest, most honourable man of my acquaintance. His character is to be valued far more than the King's coffers."

Elizabeth could not help but mutter under her breath. "Which the Prince Regent is currently spending like water through a net."

He heard. It caught him completely off guard. *She knows politics and the events of the monarchy as well?* Miss Elizabeth would have much in common with Darcy. He turned to look at his cousin and found him staring at them...at her. *Ah, the young lady has his attention.*

"Miss Elizabeth, I will be dancing the next with Miss Bennet—and Miss Bingley the set after. Might I introduce you to my cousin before the evening is over?"

Elizabeth had allowed her fertile imagination to mold this Mr. Darcy into the man of her dreams. To remain unknown, was to keep him perfect, a knight in shining armor, unblemished and unflawed. She spent the remainder of the dance pondering the introduction to come. She hoped his voice was rich, smooth, and deep.

Until this night, Elizabeth felt she knew herself well. Her father was proud of her reasonable, inquisitive mind. She had been as well. Nevertheless, since the entry of the particular gentleman from Netherfield Park, her flights of romantic fancy had been reminiscent of her youngest sisters. *She had best take charge of herself!*

"Yes, Colonel Fitzwilliam, I would be delighted to welcome your cousin to Meryton." Elizabeth could see this pleased her partner, who seemed to continue the dance with a lighter step, inconsistent with his size.

Mr. Darcy danced once with Miss Bingley and once with Mrs. Hurst, the sisters of his friend. He spent the balance of the evening walking about the room or leaning against the wall, speaking occasionally to one of his own party. As she had pondered earlier in the evening, *Was he above the present company?* Surely, with his rumoured wealth and stature, he was an accomplished man who could perform the steps needed to dance more than twice. Elizabeth wondered again, *was he shy?*

Whatever the answer, it was a disappointment to more than one young lady, as gentlemen were scarce, and several had to sit out each dance due to lack of a partner, including Elizabeth.

Elizabeth was seated with her good friend Charlotte amidst other ladies when Mr. Darcy, the colonel, and Mr. Bingley stopped adjacent to them and commenced speaking.

"Come, Darcy," said Mr. Bingley, "I must have you dance. I hate to see you standing about by yourself in this stupid manner. You had much better dance."

"I certainly shall not. You know how I detest it, unless I am particularly acquainted with my partner. At such an assembly as this, it would be insupportable. Your sisters are engaged, and there is not another woman in the room whom it would not be a punishment to me to stand up with."

Mr. Darcy ignored the glare from his cousin. Elizabeth easily recognised that look as her mother often directed the same towards her when she was displeased.

"I would not be so fastidious as you are for a kingdom!" cried Mr. Bingley. "Upon my honour, I never met with so many pleasant girls in my life, as I have this evening; and there are several of them, you see, uncommonly pretty."

"*You* are dancing with the only handsome girl in the room," said Mr. Darcy, looking at the eldest Miss Bennet. He turned to his cousin. "You, Richard, would welcome any female as a partner as long as they have two legs."

"Darcy!" The colonel hissed. He was appalled at his cousin's contemptuous attitude, though he was not surprised. It was always so at large gatherings. He gave his cousin a censorious look, then walked away.

Mr. Bingley failed to note the exchange between the two men. He only had eyes for Jane. "Oh! She is the most beautiful creature I ever beheld! But there is one of her sisters sitting down just behind you, Miss Elizabeth, who is very pretty, and I dare say very agreeable. Do let me ask my partner to introduce you."

"Which do you mean?" and turning round, he looked for a moment at the small group of young ladies sitting on either side of the woman he had noticed earlier. Focusing on the maiden whose features were somewhat similar to Miss Bennet's, he said, "She is tolerable; but not handsome enough to tempt *me*; and I am in no humour at present to give consequence to young ladies who are slighted by other men. You had better return to your partner and enjoy her smiles, for you are wasting your time with me."

Bingley longed for the floor to open up and swallow him and Darcy completely. By the pained expression on Elizabeth's face, she had heard every word uttered by his friend. He raised his eyebrows in alarm. Darcy merely stiffened and walked away.

Elizabeth gasped at his insult. *How dare he speak about me in such a manner…to be overheard by my neighbors?* In her lifetime she had never been the target of such rudeness, disdain, or arrogance. His character was now decided. *Mr. Blatantly Offensive* had fallen from his white stallion and tarnished his shining armor. He was the proudest, most disagreeable man in the world, and everybody, most especially Elizabeth Bennet, hoped he would never again be in their company. She was grateful Colonel Fitzwilliam had not yet performed an introduction.

Mr. Darcy was an enigma…until he spoke. *Then* he was the enemy.

Covered in mortification and enraged at his disparagement, Elizabeth's cheeks glowed a flaming red and fire was shooting from her eyes. Charlotte reached over and put her hand on Elizabeth's forearm when it looked like she would stand. Seeing the mixture of ire and hurt on her friend's face and hoping to gain Elizabeth's attention before she did something foolish, Charlotte asked, "Eliza, what do you think of our visitors now?" It would not surprise any person in attendance if Elizabeth stood toe-to-toe with the gentleman and shared her personal view of his character flaws. That was her way.

Nonetheless, what was also known about Elizabeth Bennet was her unfailing kindness and her ability to laugh at the ridiculous. Charlotte knew how best to placate her friend. Though there was a difference in their upbringing and education, they both appreciated the keen intellect of the other. Charlotte was much more practical than Elizabeth, who was a romantic at heart, though Elizabeth would not likely admit that to herself or anyone else.

"Does he not remind you of Farmer Glenn's peacock?" Charlotte whispered.

Elizabeth spun her head to look directly at Charlotte, the sparks turning into a twinkle. "Why, Charlotte, I do believe you are correct." Elizabeth snickered. "At any moment, he might start shaking his tail feathers and squawk. Insolent man!" The last was said with the same dour expression currently on the man's face. Both young ladies laughed with delight, completely unaware they were, again, being observed by Mr. Darcy himself.

Elizabeth cared not that he might have heard her comments. She had certainly heard his and she only regretted they were breathing the same air in the enclosed room.

"My father gave that peacock to Farmer Glenn, Charlotte." Elizabeth's smile was mixed with a hint of mischief. "Papa claims they are a vain, proud bird whose only virtue is their outer appearance. I would not be surprised if Mrs. Glenn served the miserable bird for Sunday dinner."

At that, Elizabeth looked up from where she was seated and caught his eye, refusing to look away first. He must have had the same determination. Eventually, as the music changed and the next set queued, her attention was diverted by her next partner. Mr. Darcy was off the hook— for now.

Darcy groaned to himself. She had heard and she was the daughter of *that* woman. He moved with purpose through the crowds of dancers to the far wall to take up position in the corner. His mind could not contemplate how the lovely beauty could possibly be from that ridiculous family. He sought her face and found she had turned to her friend, paying him no more attention than she did any other in the room. He dropped his head and wondered why he felt such a loss. They had not yet been introduced and he sincerely doubted she would welcome it now. He knew his actions had not been that of a gentleman, and he felt disappointment with himself—a feeling that made him most uncomfortable.

With a genuine smile, Elizabeth stood to join Mr. Bingley on the dance floor. How this man could be friends with *Mr. Sour Puss* was a conundrum.

"Miss Elizabeth, I am delighted you had this set free. Your sister, Miss Bennet, is a wonderful partner." He then blushed to his ears. "A wonderful dance partner for a certainty."

Elizabeth was charmed and vowed to think of *Mr. Exceedingly Frustrating* no more. During the dance, Mr. Bingley spoke of how much he relied on *Mr. Knows Everything* for guidance on estate matters. She realised that he might likely rely on him for personal matters as well. She did not know how easily Mr. Bingley accepted and followed such counsel.

This left Elizabeth with a dilemma. Her vow to hate *Mr. Ridiculously Rude* must be shelved as she did with the stacks of books she filed away in her father's library. She wanted nothing to come between Mr. Bingley and Jane. Nothing, not even her injury.

While Elizabeth's dance partner was distracted by Jane's progress throughout the set, she contrived the perfect strategy. Espying Miss Bingley's attempts to garner *Mr. Proud and Prejudice's* attention, Elizabeth realised her best weapon was distraction. If she could throw Miss Bingley and *Mr. Presumptuousness* together, they would be too occupied with each other to interfere with Jane's fledgling romance.

Seconds after that decision was made, the set ended and Bingley escorted her back to Jane. The colonel stepped in front of her with an apology for his tardiness. He may wear the uniform of a soldier, however, it was she who was headed for battle. Placing her hand on his arm, she recalled a quote on war strategy from an ancient Chinese philosopher. *Pretend inferiority and encourage his arrogance.*

J. DAWN KING

http://JDawnKing.com J. Dawn King @jdawnking

Compromised!

Also Available in Audiobook
Narrated by Catherine O'Brien

One Love, Two Hearts, Three Stories
A Pride and Prejudice Anthology

The Library
What happens when Fitzwilliam Darcy and Elizabeth Bennet are alone in the library at Netherfield Park and they decide to talk instead of ignore each other?

Married!
Fitzwilliam Darcy needs a wife! Elizabeth Bennet needs a husband! What results when two strong-minded, kind-hearted strangers unite in this most sacred state? Will love grow?

Ramsgate
When Miss Georgiana Darcy stumbles upon her beloved George Wickham willingly wrapped in a passionate embrace with someone else, the elopement is off. Running to her new friend, Miss Elizabeth Bennet, she involves her in a plan to get help from her brother, Fitzwilliam Darcy, and bring Wickham to justice. Enjoy this alternate path to our favorite couple's happily ever after.

Available in Trace Paperback, eBook, and Audiobook format from the following retailers:

J. DAWN KING

http://JDawnKing.com J. Dawn King @jdawnking

Men of Derbyshire Series

A Father's Sins

How do Fitzwilliam Darcy and Elizabeth Bennet overcome the consequences of poor decisions made by their fathers when Darcy and Elizabeth were young? Will love have a chance?

This is a stand-alone story.

Also Available in Spanish / También disponible en Español

Finding Their Way COMING SOON!

After Miss Jane Bennet put the needs and desires of her parents ahead of a relationship with Mr. Charles Bingley, the gentleman left his leased estate of Netherfield Park, broken-hearted, never to return. Bingley arrived in London and found his household in turmoil. His confidante and counselor, Fitzwilliam Darcy, was unavailable. What is an amiable, indecisive young man to do?

Follow along in this full-length novel as Charles Bingley and Jane Bennet travel uncharted territory to accomplishment, responsibility, accountability, maturity, and love.

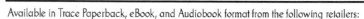

Available in Trace Paperback, eBook, and Audiobook format from the following retailers:

Made in the USA
San Bernardino, CA
19 May 2016